and observation of childr
in Liverpool with his wife and four children

Other books by the same author

# Final Countdown

## ALAN GIBBONS

A Dolphin
Paperback

First published in Great Britain in 1999
as a Dolphin paperback
by Orion Children's Books
a division of the Orion Publishing Group Ltd
Orion House
5 Upper St Martin's Lane
London WC2H 9EA

A catalogue record for this book
is available from the British Library

Typeset at The Spartan Press Ltd,
Lymington, Hants
Printed in Great Britain by
Clays Ltd, St Ives plc.

ISBN 1 85881 661 0

# Rough Diamonds

## THE SQUAD

Darren 'Daz' Kemble (goalkeeper)
Joey Bannen (defence and substitute goalkeeper)
Anthony 'Ant' Glover (defence)
Jimmy Mintoe (defence)
John O'Hara (midfield)
Jamie Moore (midfield)
Kevin 'Guv' McGovern (midfield and captain)
Bashir Gulaid (midfield)
Pete 'Ratso' Ratcliffe (midfield)
Dave Lafferty (striker)
Gordon Jones (defence)
Liam Savage (striker)
Conor Savage (striker)
Chris Power (substitute)
Dougie Long (substitute)

Manager: Ronnie Mintoe

# PART ONE

# *Hard Knocks*

*Football is suffering – and joy.*

Former Italian national coach
Cesare Maldini

# One

Kev McGovern stole an uneasy glance at the touch-line, his fifth in as many minutes. The dark, wiry man in the leather jacket was making him distinctly uneasy. What *was* Dad doing there? The doting father he wasn't. Watching his son playing Sunday morning football had never been high in the priorities of Tony McGovern. Wheeling, dealing, strong-arming maybe; but fatherhood – never. The only time Dad showed was when he was after something.

'Guv!'

At the sound of his nickname, Kev spun round on his heels. He spotted the danger immediately. The Sefton Dynamoes' winger, Alan Cross, was tearing down the left flank with real purpose. Skipping over Joey Bannen's despairing tackle, he weighed up his options. With nobody in the box to aim at, Cross turned infield and went at Ant Glover. It was a good move. In most situations Ant was a rock solid defender, but one-on-one a player with pace could turn him. Kev took it all in at a glance and sprinted back to help his disintegrating defence, all thoughts of Dad at the back of his mind.

'Cover the runner into the box,' he shouted to the advancing Chris Power. 'I've got Cross.'

Alerted to Kev's approach, Cross hesitated. There wasn't a player in the league who didn't know about Kev McGovern's tackling. A split second was all Kev needed. Gritting his teeth, he stuck out a boot and drove the ball against Cross's shins. It bounced off his opponent and ran out of play.

'Ref,' Kev roared. 'Diamonds' throw.'

Seeing the ref's arm raised in his favour, he grinned broadly.

'Yes.'

A couple of yards away, Cross was hobbling away from the tackle. The sight gave Kev even more satisfaction than the throw-in. What better than taking the ball *and* the man?

After a cruncher like that, there weren't many kids who fancied a repeat performance, and Cross certainly looked wary.

'Make a run for me somebody,' Joey was complaining as he took the throw. Kev was the first to respond. He always was. He had strong ideas about his role as team captain. Lead by example: first into the tackle, last to give up the cause. That's why they called him the Guv'nor. Bringing the ball down, he turned neatly and flicked it on to Liam Savage ahead of him.

'Return ball,' he shouted excitedly, surging past a puffing Dynamoes' defender.

Liam didn't let him down, rolling the ball neatly into his path. But Kev was under pressure from the charging Dynamoes' keeper. He had to pick his spot in the blink of an eyelid. It was all he needed. He would savour this moment later. It was sheer perfection. He didn't rush his shot. He didn't smash it. He simply adjusted his feet and stroked it under the keeper's body and into the net.

'Iceman!' declared Ratso admiringly.

'Good finish, Guv,' said Liam.

'Nice assist,' Kev answered. He was in a generous mood.

Five minutes into the second half, the Diamonds had broken the deadlock. The relief showed on his team-mates' faces. Anything short of a win, and they could kiss the South Sefton Junior League title goodbye. If the Diamonds made the slightest mistake, the leaders Longmoor Celtic would be all but uncatchable. Their second consecutive title. Kev's goal might just keep the Rough Diamonds in the hunt.

'Right, lads,' Kev urged, stabbing both index fingers at his forehead. 'Concentrate. It's only a one-goal lead. Don't get carried away.'

They'd got carried away too often this season. Sometimes it was a vendetta with the opposition. Usually it was stupid personal rivalries *within* the team.

The Diamonds could be their own worst enemies. No time for that now. It was time to stay focused. It didn't need to be pretty. They just had to grind out a result.

'Kev, Kev,' came a voice behind him.

Dad. He was giving the thumbs up. Kev smiled weakly. What *was* he after?

'Cracking goal, son. Keep it up.'

Kev didn't so much as look in his old feller's direction. Best to blot him out completely.

'Hey Kev, did you hear me?'

Kev kept his face turned. It was hard. He wanted nothing more than Dad's approval. But how many times had Dad lifted his hopes, only to dash them again? Like when he got a name torching buildings and busting lips for a living. Like when he did a vanishing act for four whole years, leaving Mum to keep the family together. Like when he finally re-surfaced only to team up with local villain Lee Ramage. Together Dad and Ramage constituted a two-man crime wave.

'What's *he* doing here?' asked Bashir, the Diamonds' winger.

He had good cause to be worried. Bashir's dad had a

shop on South Parade, right next door to the distinctly iffy taxi firm Kev's dad ran with Ramage.

'Dunno, Bash lad,' Kev replied, doing his best to sound unfazed. 'Let's get on with the game, eh?'

Bashir got on with it the best way he knew, by cutting through the Dynamoes' defence like a buzz saw. His cross only narrowly evaded Liam Savage's twin brother Conor.

'Time to turn up the heat,' Kev told his troops. 'They're there for the taking.'

Midway through the half, the Diamonds were doing everything but score. Liam and Conor both went close and Kev rattled the woodwork with a searing shot from ten yards out.

'This is just too easy,' smirked Conor.

'You can cut that out,' said Kev. 'You're never safe at one-nil.'

Conor shook his head.

'And where are this lot going to get an equalizer from?'

An own goal, that's where. Disaster struck when the Dynamoes' Phil Martin booted the ball hopefully out of defence. The speculative punt bounced over the head of Chris Power playing centre back for the Diamonds and found Alan Cross. It was the first foray he'd made into the danger area since Kev's tackle. This time he wriggled free of his marker and had the space and time to measure his pass. Cross whipped the ball in low, finding the heel of the unfortunate Joey Bannen. Completely wrong-footed by the cruel deflection, Daz Kemble in goal could only watch as the ball spun over the line.

One-one.

It was a goal that knocked the stuffing out of the

Diamonds. For the next ten minutes they were hanging on by their fingernails as the rejuvenated Dynamoes swept forward. Suddenly it was all hands to the pumps as the Diamonds' forwards came back to assist the defence. Kev was the rock on which wave after wave of attacks broke. He was at the centre of half a dozen goalmouth scrambles, clearing his lines with his boot, his head, even his knee.

'Ronnie,' he appealed after yet another frenetic melee in the Diamonds' box. 'We've got to ring the changes here. A draw's no good to us.'

He didn't even mention the other D-word. Defeat was something he didn't dare contemplate.

'I'm one step ahead of you,' said Ronnie, nodding in the direction of Jamie Moore and Gordon Jones warming up on the touch-line.

Catching the ref's attention, Ronnie pulled off Joey Bannen and John O'Hara. By the time Jamie and Gord had arrived on the pitch, Kev had begun reorganizing his beleaguered troops.

'Chris, Ant, Gord,' he ordered. 'You make a back three. Ratso, me and you will play a holding role in midfield. Jimmy, Jamie and Bashir, it's your job to squeeze up the play and give the twins some support. We're letting the Dynamoes come on to us. We've got to push up as a unit.'

'You sure this is wise?' asked Ratso. 'We'll be leaving ourselves wide open.'

'There's no point playing safe now,' said Kev. 'All the other top sides are winning their games. Anything short of the three points and we're out of the chase.'

Kev's dire warning did the trick. The news about the other title-contenders ran through the team like an electric shock. The Diamonds were soon putting together their first real attacking moves since early in the half. It was five games since Jamie's last appearance and he was hungry for success. Teaming up with Jimmy Mintoe and Conor, Jamie was part of a three-pronged assault on the Dynamoes' right flank. His chance to put himself back in contention for a place in the Diamonds' starting line-up came within minutes. A hasty clearance fell to Jamie's feet on the touch-line. Looking up, he spotted Bashir lurking unmarked on the far side of the pitch. Jamie's crossfield pass completely threw the defence.

'Bash, Bash,' yelled Liam. 'First-time ball.'

Bashir struck it on the half-volley. Liam had only to get a touch and it would be in the net. He made no mistake.

Two-one.

'You did well,' Kev told Bashir. 'That wasn't an easy ball.'

Bashir smiled, but only after he'd glared pointedly at Kev's dad.

'He's still there.'

Kev grimaced.

'I know. I didn't invite him. Honest. I just wish he'd leave me alone.'

'Then tell him,' said Bashir.

'It isn't that easy,' said Kev.

Bashir shook his head. Over the last year he'd had enough excuses from Kev to wallpaper his bedroom.

'It is, you know.'

The Diamonds regained possession right from the kick-off and surged back into attack. Kev could feel the confidence draining out of the opposition. They were like lambs to the slaughter. Taking advantage of a poor punch out by the keeper, Kev threaded the ball through a knot of defenders. It found Jamie, leaving him with the easiest of chances.

Three-one.

Right on full-time Bashir joined the roll of honour, scrambling home a corner from close range.

Four-one.

'What's this, Bash?' said Kev. 'Winger turned goal-poacher. You've made my day.'

'You could make mine,' said Bashir, stubbornly refusing to be sidetracked. 'Tell your dad to leave us alone. He's no good. He's the one who smashed up our shop. I know it, and so do you. I don't understand you. After everything he's done, how can you even speak to him?'

'You can't argue with that,' said Jamie. 'Dad or no dad, he's brought you nothing but grief. Steer clear, Kev.'

Kev turned away. They were right. He knew they were right. But since when did that matter? Stuff right and wrong. Nobody can control their feelings and so what that his dad was as crooked as an eleven-pence piece? He loved him the way an eagle loves the sky.

'Let's get on with the game,' he told them guiltily.

At the final whistle the Diamonds crowded round Kev.

'Great win,' said Ant.

'Think we've made up any ground on the leaders?' asked Gord.

'No such luck,' said Ratso, recalling Kev's earlier remark. 'With a few minutes to go all the others were winning.'

Kev gave a broad grin.

'Now what makes you say that, Rats?'

Ratso stared at him.

'But you told me . . .'

'Now how would I know the score, Rats?' asked Kev. 'I've been in the thick of the game, just like you.' He patted his shirt and shorts. 'Nowhere to keep a mobile phone is there?'

The penny dropped.

'You crafty beggar, Guv, you made it up. You only said it to make us try harder.'

Kev grinned. 'Exactly.'

'So how *did* the top teams do?' asked Daz Kemble.

'Good point,' said Kev.

'I'm on my way,' said Ratso. Without further ado, the Diamonds' in-house statistician raced off to find out. He returned two minutes later.

'What do you want first?' he asked. 'The good news or the bad news?'

'Bad news,' said John O'Hara, ever the doom and gloom merchant.

'The bad news,' Ratso announced, 'is that Ajax and the Liver Bird drew.'

'That's the bad news!' cried Kev. 'So what's the good news?'

Ratso's face almost cracked with pleasure.

'Only that Longmoor lost. One-nil to St Bede's.'

The news sent the Diamonds into hysterics, punching the air and elbowing each other gleefully. They'd closed the gap at the top to just four points. But as the celebrations subsided, Kev heard a familiar – and unwelcome – voice.

'Kev lad,' said Dad. 'Can I have a word?'

Kev exchanged glances with Bashir and Jamie.

'OK, Dad,' he said, barely able to look his mates in the eye. 'Give me a minute to change into my trainers.'

# Two

With his boots hanging laced together round his neck Kev followed Dad from the playing field to the litter-strewn car park. Like a condemned man, he thought, and Dad was his gallows.

'That mate of yours doesn't like me much, does he?' Dad asked, glancing across at the Diamonds still chatting on the pitch.

'Which one?'

'The black lad, of course, that Gulaid feller's kid. He was giving me the eye all through the match.'

Kev shrugged.

'Honestly, Dad, is it any wonder? You've been trying to put the frighteners on Mr Gulaid ever since he got the shop on the Parade. It's a wonder Bashir talks to me at all.'

'It isn't personal against old Gooly,' said Dad. 'He takes a bit too much interest in Lee and I, that's all. The coppers have been sniffing round again. Where do you think they're getting their information?'

'Well, not from Mr Gulaid,' said Kev. 'He just wants to be left alone. Besides, you wouldn't have anything to worry about if you kept it legitimate.'

'Now hang on a minute,' said Dad. 'I'll have you know the taxis are all above board. You don't have too high an opinion of your old man, do you?'

Kev shrugged. What exactly did Dad expect him to be proud of? The punch-ups, the dealing, the arson?

'That might have something to do with your track record.'

'Ouch,' said Dad. 'I suppose I asked for that. Ashamed of me, are you?'

Kev looked away. How did he answer that one? Mum definitely was, and the rest of the family hated him. After a long silence, Kev managed a mumbled reply.

'Sometimes . . . All that trouble over the shop . . . You know.'

'Sure lad, I know. But I've got to make a crust, haven't I? It's not like I left school with a pocketful of certificates.'

He clenched his fists.

'These are my qualifications.'

Kev remembered all the times he'd punched his own way out of trouble. Who was he to look down his nose at Dad? After all, they were cut from the same cloth.

'Anyway,' he said, I don't think you dragged me over here to sell me a hard-luck story. What gives?'

Dad grinned.

'Can't pull the wool over your eyes, can I, Kev? It's Jack Dougan.'

Kev's face dropped. One disaster can be an accident, but two has to be more than bad luck. Not only was his dad a villain, but his mum had started going out with a copper! Mum's Mr Plod was a sensitive issue with Dad, of course. She'd met him on a girls' night out, only to discover he was a detective sergeant and knew Dad very well indeed.

Despite everything Dad had done, somewhere inside Kev still thought he and Mum ought to be together. Stupid, fancy a hard-bitten kid like him believing in Happy Families.

'Is she still seeing him?' asked Dad.

'Dunno. He hasn't been round lately.'

'So there isn't much to tell?'

Kev frowned.

'You already know all this. I was there when you had

the big stand-up row with him. What are you after, Dad?'

Dad ran a hand over his short, stubbly hair.

'Dougan's mustard. A keen copper, and that's the worst sort. He'd love to put me inside. He's the one who's been turning up the heat. I just want to know who I'm dealing with.'

Kev snorted.

'You mean you want something to use against him. Look, Dad, you know exactly who you're dealing with. If you want to know about Mum and this Dougan feller, you'll have to ask them. Leave me out of it.'

'Whoa', said Dad, catching Kev by the arm. 'I just want to know if they're serious, or anything. Me and Carol were married for twelve years. Still are, come to think of it, at least until the divorce comes through.'

'So you're just looking after her welfare?' sneered Kev.

He'd been through all this before, so often he'd even picked up Mum's way of talking.

'Yes,' said Dad, a half-smile playing on his thin lips. 'Something like that.'

After a moment, 'Kev?'

'Yes?'

'You don't like this Dougan, do you?'

Kev reacted angrily.

'Behave, he's a copper.'

Dad laughed.

'Just wondering. You don't seem too keen to spill the beans, that's all.'

'There are no beans to spill. I hardly know him. I'm not even sure Mum means to see him again.'

It was a lie. Kev wasn't stupid, and in the short time they'd known each other Mum and Dougan seemed to have become pretty serious. Dad wasn't stupid either. He knew when somebody was lying to him.

'Anyway,' said Kev. 'Is that it? Here are my mates.'

Jamie and Bashir were approaching.

'Sure,' said Dad. 'I'll let you go now.'

Kev made as if to join Jamie and Bashir.

'Oh, one thing,' said Dad. 'I hope your Mum knows what she's letting herself in for.'

Kev stopped dead in his tracks.

'Meaning?'

'Coppers and villains' wives. Definitely frowned upon that is. I wonder if Dougan's heard of consorting with criminals?'

Kev looked at Dad. He was unsure what he was getting at.

'Let's put it this way, Kev. Jack Dougan could get himself in hot water if he hangs around Carol much longer. He might even get the sack, if I'm not mistaken. Now, we wouldn't want that, would we? Shame to spoil such a promising career.'

Leaving the comment to sink in, Dad headed for his car. Kev stared after him. You might be my dad, he thought, but sometimes you really give me the creeps.

# Three

*I wish life was like a football season. Put it this way, no matter how sticky things get, on the last day all the questions are answered, all the loose ends are tied up. You get what you deserve, and if you're champions there's no argument. You're the best. The trouble is, life isn't like that.*

I don't deserve a dad who clears off without a word, or a mum who knocks around with his worst enemy. You can't spend your whole life paying for what your parents do. It isn't fair.

At least on the football field I can make a difference. I can take a game by the scruff of the neck and control it. That's what makes me the Guv'nor. Last summer I'd made things go my way for once. I'd transformed the Diamonds from scrape-the-barrel no-hopers to future title contenders. I've even led us to a trophy, the Challenge Cup. I really fancied us as League and Cup double winners this season. But, like I said, life isn't like that. We started the season well, then we hit a rough patch. First, our defence of the Cup ended in disaster when we went out to our arch rivals, the Liver Bird. Then we slid down the table. Even when we stopped the rot we were still trailing the leaders by four points with only four games to go. Suddenly I'm staring a horrible reality in the face. We might actually finish the season empty-handed.

I've sussed the problem out. It isn't that difficult really. It's us, the players, you see, we have lives, and on a dead-beat Liverpool estate like the Diamond that means pretty tough ones. I'm asking a lot, but we've got to put aside our problems and concentrate on the game.

It's stupid. Stuff keeps getting in the way of our football. First, John and Jamie's parents split up.

Then Davey Lafferty gets snapped up by the Everton School of Excellence and Liam falls out with his twin brother Conor, who just happens to be a vital member of the side. Some of the lads even dared to be ill! Not that I've got much room to talk. My life must be the most tangled web of the lot.

There's just one difference between me and the others. I never go under. No matter how often Dad's there messing up *my life, no matter how often the Liver Bird come back to haunt me, I always come through. But with everything that's happening right now, it feels like it's about my last chance.*

*It's the final countdown.*

# Four

Kev didn't usually take much notice of the radio. The music was stupid but nowhere near as stupid as the DJs. A bunch of middle-aged geeks who'd be better running a garden centre. And Mum had the cheek to complain about the noise when he and Gareth turned the Playstation on! At least their noise made sense. It was this old song that caught Kev's attention, one of the DJ's raves from the grave (yawn). It was a load of rubbish, but the chorus struck a chord with him. *I don't like Mondays*, the divvy singer was warbling. Well, who does? Sometimes Kev felt as if he was only alive at the weekend, willing the Blues to victory on a Saturday afternoon, playing out his dreams down Jacob's Lane the following Sunday morning. Then came Monday and that meant school. No dreams at school, just a bunch of deadheads telling you what to do.

'Did you get a letter about Parents' Evening?' Mum asked.

Kev stared into his Frosties.

'Oh yeah, I forgot. It's in my blazer pocket.'

'Well, go and get it then. You should have shown it to me on Friday evening. I only know about it because Pat told me. I wish you were more like Cheryl.'

Cheryl was Kev's goody-two-shoes cousin. Top set in

everything, even looks. She wasn't thirteen yet and the older lads were trying to chat her up already.

'Here.'

Mum filled in the tear-off slip at the bottom.

'I just hope it's good news this time. The one last October was embarrassing.'

Kev grunted. What did she expect? Scarisbrick was a dump. He turned up, didn't he? Surely he wasn't expected to work as well!

'Are you listening to me?' Mum asked sharply. 'You promised to try harder. So what's Mrs Spinks going to have to say to me?'

Kev shrugged his shoulders. Who cared what old Stinks had to say?

Mum softened her tone. 'You have been trying, haven't you, love?'

Kev nodded. It was a lie though. Most of the time school just passed him by. He didn't mind technology, especially woodwork and metalwork. But they had to go and spoil it by making him do cooking as well. All the other stuff, well, it sucked.

'I get good reports, don't I?' chirped Gareth.

'Of course you do, babe,' Mum answered, tousling his hair.

'He should do,' Kev snorted. 'He's only got to spell cat and count to ten.'

'He is still six,' said Mum. 'At least he tries, which is more than I can say for his big brother.'

Kev stifled a yawn. Same old battle-lines. Didn't she ever let up?

'You're nearly thirteen, Kev. You need qualifications if you want to get on. It's not like when I was your age when kids could walk into a job.'

By now, Kev had switched off completely. He

was saved by the bell, or the trill of the phone to be exact.

'Get that for me, will you?' Mum asked. 'I've got to do Gareth's packed lunch.'

The moment Kev lifted the receiver his heart sank. It was a man's voice, gruff and nasal – Jack Dougan.

'Is your Mum there?'

Kev didn't reply. Instead he called into the kitchen.

'Mum, it's Plod.'

Mum shot him a ferocious glare.

'It wouldn't cost you anything to be civil to him.'

'Sure,' said Kev. 'Whatever.'

As Mum picked up the phone Kev remembered what Dad had said. Should he warn her?

'Jack,' she said breathlessly. 'What a lovely surprise.'

The tone of her voice banished any generous thoughts Kev might have had. Warn *her*? Help *him*? Whatever Dad did have planned for Dougan, he had it coming. As the conversation dragged on, Kev found more and more excuses to walk in and out of the kitchen, eavesdropping. Mum must have realized what he was up to. She hardly said anything worth listening to. In the end, Kev waved to her.

'I'm off.'

'Oh, see you, love. Have a nice day. And don't forget that slip for Parents' Evening.'

Kev nodded, but the slip stayed where it was, in the middle of the kitchen table.

If there was one lesson Kev hated more than any other it was French. It was the last lesson on Monday afternoons. He definitely didn't like Mondays. All he knew about France was its best players, Henry and Petit,

Zidane and Thuram. And that was all he wanted to know. He gazed longingly outside at Year Ten climbing aboard the school minibus. They were playing some school in Huyton. Jammy beggars.

'Kev,' hissed Chris. 'She's looking at you again.'

Kev looked up. Sure enough Mrs Kent was staring right at him.

'*Et toi*?' she asked.

'Come again?' Kev answered.

It hadn't been meant as a joke, but the rest of the class fell about laughing.

'I asked you,' Mrs Kent said huffily, 'the date of your birthday.'

So Kev told her. In best Scouse.

'*En français*,' said Mrs Kent. '*En français, en français,* EN FRANÇAIS.'

'Pardon?'

'Oh, do try to join in,' she said.

'Watch out,' Ratso whispered. 'She'll send you to Mr Graham.'

Graham was the Head of Year and he was in charge of discipline.

'What'll he do?' said Kev. 'Detention – big deal.'

That's when Kev remembered what Mum had said over breakfast: *It's Parents' Evening next week. There had better be some good news.* He'd had enough rows with Mum over this Dougan character. He didn't need any more. Mrs Kent was still looking at him.

'Sorry,' grunted Kev.

'Apology accepted,' said Mrs Kent. '*Et maintenant. Mon anniversaire est le vingt-deux juin. Et toi?*'

The question was directed at Ratso. She was on safer ground with him. Ratso replied in perfect singsong French. Kev flipped open his jotter, Ratso hadn't let him down. He'd drawn up the new league table ready for the training session that evening:

|  | Pl | W | D | L | Pts |
|---|---|---|---|---|---|
| Longmoor Celtic | 18 | 11 | 4 | 3 | 37 |
| Ajax Aintree | 18 | 10 | 6 | 2 | 36 |
| Liver Bird | 18 | 10 | 4 | 4 | 34 |
| Rough Diamonds | 18 | 10 | 3 | 5 | 33 |
| Northend United | 18 | 9 | 6 | 3 | 33 |
| St Patrick's Thistle | 18 | 9 | 4 | 5 | 31 |

At first reading Kev felt a surge of excitement. Four points behind the champions, Longmoor. It was nothing. They'd do it. Easy! But on second reading, the obstacles started to mount. There were six teams in the hunt, and only six points separated them. A one in six chance. Suddenly he didn't feel quite so confident. Four points behind Longmoor and only four games to go. All the front-runners had to do was keep on winning and the title was theirs. Ah, but the Diamonds still had Longmoor to play. That would be a match and a half – a six pointer. But just when Kev was beginning to feel better he remembered the rest of their fixtures. Warbreck shouldn't be much of a problem. Third from bottom, they were. But the other three matches were a minefield. There were clashes with fifth-placed Northend United and – mother and father of all battles – a last day showdown with their arch rivals, the Liver Bird, as well as the Longmoor match to go. Kev scribbled the names on Ratso's jotter. The Diamonds' last three matches were all against top-flight opposition. It was easily the hardest run-in of any of the championship hopefuls. He was just doodling a Liver Bird gravestone when a hand snatched the jotter from him.

'So this is why you're not paying attention', said Mrs Kent. 'Rough Diamonds, Celtic, Ajax. I'm keeping this until the end of the lesson. The last thing you need is anything to distract you.'

She glanced at the page. 'What is all this anyway?'

'It's our Sunday league team,' Kev explained.

'And which are you?' asked Mrs Kent.

'Rough Diamonds,' Kev replied.

'Ah,' said Mrs Kent, 'I might have guessed.'

This time it was the girls who started laughing. Kev knew from her tone of voice she was making fun of him.

'What do you think you're laughing at?' he snarled at his classmates.

'Now, now,' said Mrs Kent. 'That'll do. It was only a joke.'

'You're the joke,' Kev retorted.

'I said,' Mrs Kent repeated, 'that'll do.'

'No,' said Kev stubbornly, 'it won't. What right have you got to make fun of me?'

'Kevin,' said Mrs Kent, 'we'll have a word at the end of the lesson. Now let's get on with what we were doing.'

She was on her way back to the front of the classroom when Kev saw a couple of girls smirking at him. That did it.

'What do you think you're looking at?' he demanded angrily. He took particular exception to Karen Sargent. 'What's up with you, fat face?'

At that, Mrs Kent's patience snapped. Karen was one of her blue-eyed girls, top in French and always really keen.

'Here,' she said, slapping a disruption slip on the desk. 'Take that to Mr Graham. We'll see what he has to say about your attitude.'

Kev was already a powder keg as he made his way to

— 21 —

Mr Graham's room. He was angry with Mrs Kent, but nowhere near as angry as he was with himself. Why couldn't he keep his mouth shut? Once she found out about this, Mum would be on his back again. But, as he walked down the corridor leading to Mr Graham's room, Kev's bad day took a turn for the worse. Who should be waiting for Mr Graham but two of the Liver Bird's leading lights, his most hated enemies, Luke Costello and Andy 'Brain Damage' Ramage.

## Five

'Well,' said Costello, a smirk spreading across his face. 'Look who it isn't, the Little Matchboy.'

Kev stiffened. Trust him to bring *that* up. Kev had one thing in common with Costello – *only* one thing. They'd grown up in the same Kirkdale streets and moved up to the Diamond within months of each other. But that's where the similarities ended. The Costellos pulled up roots because the Council offered them a bigger house. Kev, however, had had no choice about the move. He'd taken it badly when Dad cleared off, and by the time he was ten he'd become a ball of raw anger. For years he was completely out of control. Mum's control. *His own* control. He took to starting fires. A chip off the rotten old block, people said. He never meant to hurt anybody, but that's exactly what he did. Kev had been one of a group of boys who used to hang around the old people's bungalows.

They plagued one old man in particular. He was frail and easy to annoy. The fire in his garden was meant as a wind-up, but it got out of hand and Kev and his mates

fled. While they were escaping through the
the fire spread to the shed where the old gu
pigeons. He was trying to save his birds when
got too much for him. He suffered a massive
attack. Unbeknown to anyone, he collapsed and ____ed.
The tragedy sent Kev's life into freefall. First, it was
threats from the neighbours, then being sent to Coventry at school and finally anonymous phone calls and
things thrown through the windows. Eventually Mum
had no choice but to move the family away. They'd
hoped for a new start, but the arrival of the Costellos put
paid to that particular dream. Now everybody on the
Diamond knew about Kev's past. For a moment the
memories were too much to bear. Kev closed his eyes,
fighting back the tears.

But he flatly refused to buckle. *I never go under.*

'Shut it, Costello,' he said, planting himself on the
other side of the corridor.

'Aw, what's the matter?' asked Brain Damage. 'Don't
you love us any more?'

'Behave,' Kev replied. 'Your own mother wouldn't
love you.'

Brain Damage scowled. Not a brain cell stirred. He
couldn't think of a single thing to say in reply.

'So what have you been up to?' asked Costello.

'Nothing,' said Kev.

'Yeah yeah, listen to Mr Innocent. You think you're
so superior, but you must have done something.'

Kev was aware of Mr Graham reading the riot act to
somebody on the other side of the door.

'OK, so I was cheeky to Mrs Kent. What did you do?'

'None of your business, McGovern.'

Costello and Brain Damage were staring at him,
trying to wind him up. He didn't flinch or turn away.

,ust returned their look with an even, unblinking glare. The tension was broken by the appearance of a boy in his cousin Cheryl's class. He had just left Graham and looked shaken by the experience.

'Looks like it's us next, Andy,' said Costello.

Andy yawned.

'I hope he's quick,' he said. 'It's nearly hometime.'

Kev listened as Mr Graham's door closed behind them. He leant the back of his head against the cracked, off-white paintwork and waited his turn. He could hear Mr Graham's raised voice, but he couldn't make out what he was saying. Every time somebody walked down the corridor they gave Kev an inquiring look: *I wonder what he's done.*

It was a quarter to three by the time Brain Damage and Costello appeared.

'You took your time,' said Kev.

'Graham's been trying to make us cough,' Costello told him. He raised his voice. He wanted Mr Graham to hear. 'He didn't get us to crack, though.'

'Whew,' said Kev sarcastically. 'Tough guy.'

Costello bristled for a few moments, then turned to Brain Damage. 'Come on, Andy. Let's get down the Parade. I want to see the fun.'

'Fun,' said Kev. 'What fun?'

'Oh nothing,' said Brain Damage, taking up where Costello had left off. 'Just something our Lee said about relocating one of the shops.'

It was the Gulaids' shop. It had to be. And if Lee Ramage was involved so was Dad. Kev remembered Dad's track record. Suddenly he could almost smell burning.

'What's going on?' Kev demanded. 'What are you on about?'

Costello winked at Brain Damage.

'Wouldn't he like to know?'

This drew an appreciative guffaw from Brain Damage.

'Come on,' said Kev. 'Spit it out. I want to know what your sleazeball brother's up to.'

'My brother,' chuckled Brain Damage. '*And* your old man. You may not like it, but they're a team. Don't forget that.'

Their goading had brought Kev to the brink.

'Tell me what's going on,' he warned. 'Or I'll . . .'

'Or you'll what?' asked Costello. 'There's two of us, McGovern.'

'You never know,' said Brain Damage slyly. 'He might call the coppers.'

'No need,' said Costello, catching his drift. 'I hear McGovern's old lady's got her own personal hot line.'

That was too much for Kev to take. Without another word, he crashed his fist into Costello's face, bouncing him back against the wall. Brain Damage was shaping up to join in the fray when Mr Graham burst out of his room.

'What on earth is going on here?'

'It was him,' cried Costello, nursing a bloody nose. 'He just went for me.'

'That's right,' said Brain Damage. 'For nothing. He's off his head, a complete psycho.'

Mr Graham listened sceptically to their version of events.

'You two get back to class,' he said. 'And clean up that nose on the way, Luke Costello. I doubt whether you're the innocent victim you make out. As for you,' he was looking directly into Kev's eyes, 'I'd have thought you were in enough trouble already. Get inside.'

*

'OK, Kevin,' said Mr Graham. 'Let's hear it.'

Kev fidgeted with his cuffs.

'He was skitting me.'

'So you hit him?'

Kev nodded.

'Getting a bit too fond of using your fists, aren't you, Kevin? That's two fights this month. Both with Mr Costello and Mr Ramage, I believe.'

'You know they were,' said Kev.

'So what's going on?'

Kev shrugged his shoulders. If there's one thing he didn't do, it was grass, not even on those two.

'Very well,' said Mr Graham. 'If you don't want to talk about what happened in the corridor, maybe you could explain your behaviour in Mrs Kent's classroom.'

'I was messing about, that's all.'

'Any particular reason?'

'No, just messing.'

'Well,' said Mr Graham, 'we don't have messing about in this school.' He pointed to a laminated poster of the school rules hanging on the wall. 'Have you read this document lately?'

Kev stared at the desk.

'Now listen to me, Kevin,' Mr Graham continued. 'You can do better. You've done better. A few months ago I really thought you'd turned over a new leaf. So did Mrs Spinks. Now this.'

Kev continued staring at the desk.

'So what have you got to say for yourself?'

Kev gave another shrug of his shoulders.

Mr Graham opened a foolscap folder. 'I'm going to have to give you a letter to take home,' he said. 'I want your mother to make a special appointment to see me on

Parents' Evening. If this nonsense doesn't stop, you're going to find yourself suspended.'

The word hit Kev like a punch in the ribs, but he didn't let it show.

'And just in case you're thinking of putting this in the bin,' Mr Graham concluded, 'there's a tear-off slip. If I don't hear from your mother I will be contacting her directly. Is that understood?'

Kev nodded. It was understood, all right. He'd messed up. Good style.

## Six

As Kev trudged out of school fifteen minutes later, he had a decision to make. Go home and face the music, or get down to South Parade and see if Costello and Brain Damage had been telling the truth about the shop. It was no contest.

'Where are you off to, Guv?' said Jamie.

'The Parade.'

'Why, what gives?'

As they crossed the busy main road, Kev filled Jamie in.

'They're just winding you up,' said Jamie. 'Any money.'

'But what if it's true?'

Jamie gave his friend a long hard look.

'OK, I'll come with you.'

As they turned into South Parade, the boys spotted Brain Damage and Costello hanging round Ramage Taxis. They'd obviously been waiting for Kev to turn up.

'Well well, if it isn't the cavalry,' hooted Costello, delighted that Kev had taken the bait.

'Come to rescue Gooly and his old man, have you?'

Kev frowned. Maybe this was a mistake. Brain Damage and Costello liked their little games of cat and mouse. It was just their style, getting him all wound up over nothing. As Kev followed Jamie into the shop he could hear their mocking laughter.

'Hello Kevin, Jamie,' said Mr Gulaid from behind the counter. 'Are you look for Bashir?'

Kev nodded.

'He could be a bit later than usual. It was their school trip today.'

Bashir was a year younger than Kev and Jamie and he was still at Cropper Lane Juniors.

'You don't mind us hanging around, do you?'

'Not at all. In fact, you can make yourselves useful.'

'Sure, what do you want us to do?'

Mr Gulaid indicated dozens of cans strewn around the floor.

'It would be a help if you could put that lot back on the shelves. Those boys just knocked them off.'

He pointed in the direction of Costello and Brain Damage.

'Does that happen much?'

Mr Gulaid nodded.

'I've barred them from the shop but they still sneak back in. It doesn't bother me that much. Just a childish prank.'

Kev and Jamie exchanged glances. It wasn't Brain Damage Mr Gulaid had to worry about; it was his older brother, Lee. They had just finished tidying the cans when they heard raised voices. Kev stiffened. Was this it, the trouble Costello and Brain Damage had promised?

'Let's take a butchers,' said Jamie.

From the doorway they could see Mr McGaw, the newsagent from further down the Parade. He was yelling at Brain Damage and Costello. Mr Gulaid joined Kev and Jamie.

'Those two again,' he sighed. 'They're always up to mischief.'

Mr McGaw was about to return to his shop, when Costello said something. Infuriated, Mr McGaw spun round and advanced on the two boys. It was at that very moment that Dad put in an appearance. He arrived with Lee Ramage in their gleaming white BMW. The car braked so quickly it sent up a puff of grey smoke from the tyres.

'Now, you can stop right there,' said Ramage, stepping out of the car. 'That's my brother you're threatening.'

'I wasn't threatening him,' panted Mr McGaw. 'He swore at me. And he's been thieving from my shop.'

'You can't prove it,' said Ramage.

Mr McGaw looked first at Ramage and then at Kev's dad.

'They took a couple of Mars bars. I saw them.'

'So where are they?' asked Ramage.

'They've eaten them, of course,' said Mr McGaw. 'Stuffed the lot in.'

Ramage was grinning. 'So show me the wrappers.'

Mr McGaw was at the end of his tether. 'They'll have thrown them away by now, as you very well know.'

Ramage thrust his face close to Mr McGaw. Kev's dad stood at Ramage's shoulder, his arms folded menacingly.

'Listen to me,' Ramage said quietly. 'You lay a finger on my kid brother and you'll have me to deal with.'

Mr McGaw's face went white. Not just with fright, but also with frustrated anger.

'Now,' Ramage concluded. 'Tell Andy you're sorry and we'll forget all about it.'

'Sorry,' exclaimed Mr McGaw. 'I'm not saying sorry to that light-fingered little . . .'

Ramage raised a hand in front of Mr McGaw's face. 'I'd watch what you said, if I were you.' That was too much for Mr McGaw. Intimidated as he was by the two younger men, he couldn't let the comment pass. 'Don't threaten me. I'm not scared of you. I know all about the likes of you. That's not a taxi firm you're running. You're just a common . . .'

Kev knew Mr McGaw had gone too far and watched as Dad seized his arm roughly.

'I think you've said enough. Now be a good boy and get back in your shop.'

Mr McGaw hesitated. It was the cue for Mr Gulaid to join in.

'How dare you talk to him like that!' he said. 'He's old enough to be your father.'

Kev's dad turned, immediately spotting Kev at Mr Gulaid's side.

'This has got nothing to do with you,' said Dad, his eyes not leaving Kev.

'Oh yes, it does,' said Mr Gulaid. 'There has been nothing but trouble since you pair opened your *business* on the Parade.'

'Meaning?'

'I think you understand my meaning.'

Without even a word to Kev, Dad locked and alarmed

the BMW and accompanied Ramage to the taxi firm next door to Mr Gulaid's shop.

'You think there's been trouble,' said Ramage. 'You ain't seen nothing yet.'

Dad said nothing but Kev could feel his eyes burning into him.

Half an hour after Dad, Kev had to face Mum. Dad's eyes had been cold and hostile. Hers were disappointed and brimming with tears. A few weeks ago she would have lit up a cigarette, but she'd given up. Not for Kev and Gareth, despite all their pleading. She'd done it for Dougan.

'Oh Kev,' she groaned, laying Mr Graham's letter face down on the kitchen table. 'How could you? You promised me you were going to make an effort.'

'I have,' said Kev, before changing it to: 'I did, for a while.'

'So what happened?'

'Dunno.'

'No,' Mum insisted. 'That isn't good enough. If you really have been working and keeping out of trouble, I want to know what's happened to make you go back to your old ways.'

Kev picked at the cloth on the table in front of him. 'Leave it, eh?'

Mum was incensed. 'Leave it? You bring this home,' she brandished the letter, 'and you tell me to leave it!'

'I got fed up, that's all. I just don't like school.'

Mum stabbed at the letter.

'I know that much,' she said. 'I've got to go and see your Head of Year. The question is: why?'

Kev shifted his feet.

'Sorry, Mum.'

'No, Kev,' she said. 'This time *sorry* just isn't good enough.'

Kev could almost feel his flesh creeping. What did she want from him?'

'I'm waiting.'

Kev wanted to scream. What was the point of going on at him like this?

'Don't you understand, Kev?' she asked, lowering her voice. 'This is important.'

Kev walked over to the fridge and went to open it. It's not that he wanted a glass of milk. It was something to do, that's all.

'What do you think you're doing?' Mum demanded. 'How can you eat at a time like this?'

'I wasn't eating,' Kev told her. 'I wanted a drink.'

'The point is,' Mum seethed, 'that I want you to pay attention to what I'm saying.'

Kev sighed and took a step back from the fridge.

'Next week,' Mum continued, satisfied that he was listening. 'I've got to go into school and give them some sort of explanation. The trouble is, Kev, I don't understand it myself.'

'Then that makes two of us,' said Kev.

'Don't be flippant!' yelled Mum. She was almost screaming.

Kev felt a hot rush through his body. Shock, humiliation, a bit of both probably.

'I can see I'm not getting through to you,' Mum said finally. 'Well, if reasoning doesn't have any effect and pleading doesn't, then I'll try something else. You're grounded.'

'But it's Monday night,' Kev protested. 'It's training.'

'*Was* training.'

'But Mum.'

'But nothing.'

Kev knew any further argument was pointless.

'Can't I at least phone Ronnie?' he asked. 'I'll have to make up some sort of excuse.'

Mum folded her arms. 'You should have thought about that before you misbehaved at school,' she said. 'Now get up to your room and stay there. If you've got anything to say to me, I'll be right here waiting.'

# Seven

*I wasn't making it up. I really don't know why I can't get on with my work at school. I mean, it isn't all that hard. And I'm not in the top set, or anything, not like Cheryl. I could muddle through though, nothing special, but enough to keep Mum off my back. So why don't I? It isn't just school either. What did I have to go down to the Parade for? I should have known Costello and Brain Damage were only winding me up. For goodness' sake, if Lee Ramage really was going to do something to the Gulaids' shop, he wouldn't let on to his blabber-mouth brother, would he? Brain Damage has got him into trouble more than once. What is the matter with me? I seem to invite trouble.*

*I'm really worried what this'll do to the Diamonds. What are the other lads going to think when I go missing without so much as a word? When I think of all the crises we've been through this season, I've always been the one who came through, the one who kept the other players going. But they're not the problem any more. This time it's me.*

# Eight

Another Sunday morning, another downpour. It was a great summer for ducks. Otherwise, the only happy people on the streets that gloomy day in late June had to be sub-aquatic. To cap it all, Ratso was doing a roaring trade in recycled one-liners.

'A few more weeks of this,' he announced to his team-mates, 'and we'll need gills to play footy.'

'Yes,' John O'Hara agreed. 'This summer's been rubbish. It was throwing it down when we went to Alton Towers with school. We had to wait for an hour in pouring rain to go on Oblivion.'

'I know,' said Ratso. 'Fins ain't what they used to be. The scales have certainly fallen from my eyes. It's been a cod awful month . . .'

'OK OK,' groaned Gord. 'Enough with the fish jokes.'

Ratso winked and slotted a cassette into his ghetto blaster. The Diamonds were skipping about, waiting to take the field to the strains of one of Ratso's repertoire of anthems.

'So what have you got for us this week?' asked Liam.

'With four games to go there's only one candidate,' said Ratso. 'No swopping and changing from now on. We're going with the same music every week.'

As the first bars of *The Final Countdown* crashed out of the ghetto blaster, the others nodded their approval. It was perfect.

'I can't see this lot giving us much of a problem, Guv,' said Jamie, weighing up the opposition.

There was no answer. Kev was preoccupied. Though almost a week had passed since that terrible Monday, he was still in the doghouse over his behaviour at school and he was continuing to worry about Dad and Lee Ramage's interest in Mr Gulaid's shop.

Those two worries alone would be enough to give anyone pause for thought. But that wasn't all. In the eyes of his team-mates he'd committed the greatest sin of all, skipping training without an excuse. Nobody had actually said anything to him. With Kev's temper, they didn't dare. But there was a definite tension in the air. Kev had let them down. If Guv could go missing, could they count on anything?

'Are you all right?' asked Jamie.

'Me? Sure, why wouldn't I be?'

Kev's studied nonchalance didn't fool Jamie. Kev was upset, and it showed.

'The ref's whistling,' said Jamie. 'He wants you in the centre circle.'

Kev nodded and made his way to the centre. The Diamonds were starting with the side that had finished the Sefton Dynamoes match, Gordon Jones replacing Joey Bannen in defence and Jamie playing wide on the right.

'Heads or tails?' asked the ref.

'Heads,' said Kev.

It was tails.

'We'll have kick-off,' said the Warbreck skipper.

Five minutes into the match, Kev knew that this was going to be no walkover. They might be third from the bottom, but Warbreck were getting the whole team behind the ball and fighting for every yard of possession. What's more, the Diamonds were definitely having an off day. Passes were going astray with depressing regularity and they'd lost their usual inventiveness. Instead of using their pace on the flanks they seemed obsessed with squeezing the ball through non-existent gaps in a packed midfield. Then came the bad news. Kev was gathering the ball for a throw-in when he heard a roar from the neighbouring pitch. It was Costello. The Liver Bird had just taken the lead in their match against Orrell Park Rangers.

Distracted by Costello's triumphant sprint downfield, Kev threw the ball straight to a grateful Warbreck defender.

'What are you playing at, Guv?' asked an exasperated Conor Savage. 'Get your mind on the game.'

Kev tried but his mind was an open door and his problems kept walking in uninvited. Every time Dad's face flashed through his mind, Bashir's followed. Just bearing the name McGovern seemed a betrayal of his friend. Midway through the first half, the Diamonds had stepped up a gear. Shaking off their early sluggishness, the wide men began to put Warbreck under pressure with some threatening runs. First Bashir got to the bye-line, releasing a great cross into the goalmouth which Conor headed narrowly over the bar. Seconds later Jamie got into the act, screwing the ball back for Kev to hit the side netting.

'More like it,' said Ratso.

Kev gave a cursory nod. The moves had been promising all right, but two half-chances wasn't much to shout about.

'You're right,' he conceded eventually. 'We just have to keep pressing.'

And press they did, but with precious little penetration. The Warbreck defence continued to soak up the punishment without ever really looking like cracking. Though the Diamonds were forcing the pace, their approach play was just too predictable. It was five minutes to the interval before Warbreck finally slipped up, and it was in freakish circumstances. Conor was playing his usual pressure game, jumping to block the keeper as he went to clear, when the keeper miscued and toe-poked the ball straight to Bashir who was lurking hopefully on the left touch-line. Desperate to make up for his mistake, the keeper charged recklessly at the advancing Bashir, who took advantage and chipped the ball over his head to Conor waiting hopefully on the edge of the area.

Faced with only one defender, Conor had no difficulty in sidestepping his man and rolling the ball into the empty net.

One-nil to the Diamonds.

When the whistle blew a few minutes later, Kev was approached by a delighted Jamie Moore.

'We'll pick up the three points now,' he said. 'Bound to.'

For the second time that morning Kev thought it over for almost a minute before answering:

'I hope you're right, Jamie.'

Jamie stood scratching his head as Kev made for the touch-line. The Guv'nor was definitely out of sorts.

The Diamonds took the field for the second half, their ears still burning from the tongue-lashing Ronnie had given them over their attitude. Kev brought to mind just a few of the choicest highlights from the team talk:

* *About as much commitment as a blancmange.*
* *I've seen lettuces with more fight.*
* *All the tactical sense of a stick of rhubarb.*

Worst of all he'd singled Kev out for particular attention. What was it he'd said? Oh yes:

* *Donkeys led by a mule.*

It wasn't like Ronnie to let rip like that, but he was aware of the tension. He was also tired.

'Look lads,' he said. 'I came straight here from the night shift.' Ronnie was a fireman at the local station, Haddon Hill. 'I could have been in bed hours ago, so how's about giving me something to stay up for?'

Easier said than done, thought Kev as he re-ran the first half in his mind. Ronnie had a point, all right. They'd been awful, and to go in one-nil up was a travesty. They'd put nothing into the game, and deserved nothing out of it.

'I've got the half-times from the other games,' Ratso told him as they limbered up.

'Go on,' said Kev. 'Let's hear it.'

'Longmoor are beating St Pat's two-nil, Ajax are walloping Blessed Hearts four-one and Liver Bird are still one-nil up against Orrell Park.'

Kev digested the information in grim silence. So their main opponents were all winning.

'Should I tell the others?' Ratso asked. 'Might be just what we need to give us a kick up the pants.'

'If you like,' said Kev.

Neither Ronnie's half-time rocket nor the news from the other pitches had any effect on his mood. Of course he wanted to snap out of it, but it was as if there were two Kev McGoverns, the real one who was aching to bury Warbreck and bring the title closer, and this pathetic replica who was allowing the match to pass him by. Right now, the replica was calling the shots.

'Come on, lads,' somebody was shouting. 'Let's get another goal to make this safe.'

It was Liam. He was doing the skipper's job, stalking round the players shouting encouragement. And the real captain? He was re-living the last few days and wincing with pain at every memory: Mum with Jack Dougan; Mum again, this time shaking her head in disappointment at Kev's letter from school; Dad threatening Mr McGaw and Mr Gulaid; last of all, Dad's eyes burning into his. Kev felt utterly overwhelmed. He wasn't the only one. For the Diamonds it was panic stations as they battled to keep Warbreck out. They had a corner.

'Come on, Kev,' Jimmy pleaded. 'Snap out of it, will you? We need you.'

Kev nodded and got ready to defend the corner. It was whipped in fast to the near post. Gord got in a diving header. Another corner. This time it was flighted to the back post. Seeing the Warbreck striker rising to meet it, Kev plunged forward. It was time to make amends for going walkabout. The move backfired. Colliding with a forward, he conceded a penalty.

'Oh classic, Guv,' groaned Ant.

'Mm,' mused Jimmy. 'Not quite what I had in mind.'

Kev walked to the edge of the penalty area, his neck burning with shame. He looked at Daz crouching on the line. Maybe the big Diamonds' keeper could pull something out of the bag and spare Kev's blushes.

'Come on, Daz,' he hissed. 'You can do it.'

The penalty was struck at catchable height, but it was well placed, just inside the left-hand post. Daz dived the right way, succeeding in getting his fingers to the ball. It wasn't enough, however. There was power in the shot and Daz could only push it against the post. From there it spun agonizingly into the net.

One-one.

'That was rash, McGovern,' snarled Daz. 'You played like a div.'

Not *Guv*, but McGovern. Kev knew what the lads

were thinking. Missing Monday, playing rubbish this morning. Maybe the Guv'nor really had lost it.

Warbreck had seized the initiative and they weren't about to sit on their laurels. Winning back possession, they came swarming into attack. Only a flying save by Daz stopped them taking the lead. Kev glanced at the touch-line where John was warming up. A substitution seemed imminent. But who was he going to replace? That's when Kev caught Ronnie's eye. Surely not. He was the captain, the Guv'nor.

Jamie must have read Kev's mind. Or Ronnie's. 'You'd better do something, Guv. Quick.'

Kev had never had a better incentive to get stuck in. He met the corner with a strong header and watched with satisfaction as Bashir collected it and raced upfield. Two minutes later he broke up a menacing Warbreck attack with a biting tackle. He risked another look at the bench. John had sat back down. Kev had done enough to earn a reprieve.

'A draw's not good enough,' panted Ratso next to him. 'I've just checked with Ronnie. The top three are still winning. If we don't pull this out of the fire, they'll extend their lead over us.'

'Over my dead body,' said Kev. The Guv'nor was back.

Spotting a Warbreck player floundering in surface water near the centre circle, Kev threw himself into the challenge. In a spray of rainwater, he dispossessed his man and came away with the ball. Taking in the forward players' positions at a glance, he decided to run with it. Warbreck's marking was as tight as ever.

'Guv, Guv,' Conor and Liam were shouting.

'Guv,' Jamie begged.

But they were all being watched too closely. He

needed another outlet. It came in the form of Bashir helpfully scampering infield. Kev got his foot round the ball and guided it into Bashir's path. Knowing that he still had to prise open the Warbreck defence, Kev drove forward, tussling with the centre back before spinning off him into space.

'Bash,' he cried, seeing the opportunity. 'Through ball. Now!'

Bashir hit the ball first time. Meeting it on the half-volley, Kev swept the crisp pass into the net.

'Yiss!'

Two-one to the Diamonds.

Punching the air, Kev turned to receive the accolades of the rest of the team.

'Screamer!' Ratso bawled approvingly.

'Good strike,' said Conor.

'More like the old Guv,' said Jamie with a grin.

But the job wasn't done yet. Incensed at what they saw as a fluke against the run of play, Warbreck laid siege to the Diamonds' goal. A series of solid defensive headers and clearances by Ant and Chris held the line for the Diamonds, but still Warbreck powered forward. With a minute to go, it looked as if the Diamonds had finally weathered the storm when Jimmy slipped, letting in the Warbreck winger.

'Oh no, not now!' groaned Kev, stranded twenty yards from the danger area, too far away to be of any help.

Daz rushed the attacker, standing tall and spreading his arms. Kev couldn't be of any use in stopping the winger, but maybe, just maybe he could make it to the line. The Warbreck attacker slid the ball under Daz's flailing gloves and hurdled the diving keeper. He only had to stay on his feet to score. Kev forced every ounce of energy into the last few strides which would take him to the line and a heroic clearance. The winger put in his shot, a side-footed effort that was short on pace but low and accurate. Kev stuck out a boot and managed to hook the ball into the air. As he sprawled on the greasy turf he saw the ball rising. It struck the bar and cannoned back down. As the Warbreck players claimed a goal, Gord scooped the loose ball out of play.

'No goal,' yelled Kev, scrambling to his feet. 'It didn't cross the line. Never on this earth.'

There were tears in his eyes. He hadn't blown it. He couldn't have done.

'On, come on, ref,' Kev pleaded. 'You know what you saw. The clearance was good. No goal.'

'What do you mean, no goal?' asked the nearest Warbreck player. 'It was definitely over the line.'

'Ask anybody,' Kev said, waving his arms at the knot of spectators. 'They'll tell you.'

'Tell us what?' said the Warbreck player. 'It was a goal, fair and square.'

'Behave,' said Daz, joining the argument. 'It didn't cross the line, not all of it.'

The ref frowned and stared at the patch of studded turf where mud almost obscured the line. It was as if he was trying to conjure up his own action replay.

'You've got to be joking,' groaned the Warbreck winger whose shot had been diverted on to the bar. 'You can't be taking them seriously, ref.'

The ref continued to stare at the line, then raised both hands above his head, signalling a throw-in. It was no goal. Ninety seconds later he blew for full-time. Warbreck were gutted. The Diamonds were elated.

'Brilliant clearance,' said Daz, slapping Kev on the back. 'That made up for the earlier cock-up.'

'There's just one problem,' Kev whispered, a mischievous smile crossing his face. 'That shot, it did cross the line.'

'You're kidding,' said Daz. 'You were dead convincing. You deserve an Oscar for your performance.'

Kev looked at the storm clouds scudding across the leaden sky. For the first time that morning he wasn't haunted by Mum, Dad, school, anything.

'Don't I just?' he chuckled.

## Nine

But Kev's day of twists and turns wasn't over yet. Flushed from the Diamonds' skin-of-the-teeth victory over Warbreck, he almost floated through the back door.

'Mum,' he shouted. 'I'm back.'

But as he walked into the kitchen he felt suddenly apprehensive. For a start it was quiet. It was never quiet in his house. Mum always had the radio on, even when she was out of the room.

Then there was the real sickener. On the kitchen surface there was an ashtry and in the ashtray a cigarette stub was still smouldering. She was smoking again! She'd chain-smoked for years, but had given up for Dougan. That's what happiness had done for her. This could only mean one thing.

'Mum,' he called, the panic rising in his voice. 'Where are you?'

He was met in the corridor by Gareth.

'She's in there,' Gareth told him, pointing towards the living room. 'But she looks funny. What's the matter with her, Kev? She won't tell me.'

'I don't know, Gareth,' said Kev, his anxiety mounting. 'Honest I don't. You wait in the kitchen. I'll have a word with her.'

Waving Gareth into the kitchen, Kev took a few steps towards the living room. It was quiet there too. No telly! He glanced at his watch. It was *Jerry Springer* too. Mum never missed it. It was her way of telling herself there were people whose lives were more messed up than hers.

'Mum,' he said, edging round the door as if making his way across a minefield. 'Are you OK?'

There is one answer you just don't give to a question like that, but it was the one Mum gave.

'No, Kev,' she replied. 'I'm not all right.'

Kev stood in front of her, staring down at the top of her head. That was what scared him – she didn't even look up at him.

'Is it the school again?' he asked. 'Have they got in touch with you?'

He couldn't imagine why. He'd been making an effort ever since Mr Graham's letter. But if it wasn't him, what was it?

'No,' said Mum. 'It isn't school.'

'Then what is it? Come on, Mum, you're scaring me. And Gareth.'

This time Mum did raise her head. Her face was red, her eyes raw with crying. She looked lined and hard.

'It's your dad,' she said, by way of explanation. 'I didn't think he could hurt me any more, but he's done it again. Yes, he's really done it this time. I didn't think even he could stoop so low.'

'But what's he done?'

'Jack came round half an hour ago . . .'

'Oh,' said Kev dully. 'Him.'

'Yes,' Mum retorted. 'Him, the first man who's made

— 44 —

me feel happy in years. Well, your dad's put paid to that.'

'What do you mean?'

'There was an anonymous phone call to Jack's boss, telling them about me. It was Tony, of course. I know it was. Did you know there are rules? The police aren't supposed to get involved with villains' wives.' She laughed humourlessly. 'I bet you didn't know that's what I am, a villain's wife? Fool that I am, it didn't even occur to me that it was a problem. That's right, I've never done a thing wrong. I've never even dropped a crisp packet on the pavement. But I'm still a villain's wife. All the years we've been separated and that's what really matters, that I'm Tony McGovern's wife.'

Remembering Dad's threats, Kev ached inside. So he hadn't been bluffing. He did know how to get at Dougan.

'But I still don't understand what's happened,' said Kev. 'What's one phone call?'

'What's one phone call? I'll tell you, Kev. I'll tell you exactly what your beloved dad has done to me.'

Kev shrank back before the fury in Mum's voice.

'Jack's been transferred to Southport. That's right, miles away. And that isn't all. He's got to break it off with me, or he's out of the Force. Oh, your dad knew what he was doing all right. He hated Jack for what he was and he hated seeing me so happy. Now he's got at both of us with one little phone call.'

Kev hung his head. 'I didn't know this was what he meant,' he murmured.

Mum sat up as if jolted to attention by an electric shock.

'What?'

Kev immediately regretted saying anything.

'What did you say, Kev?'

'I said I didn't realize what he was going to do. Honest, Mum. I really didn't.'

Mum stared at him for half a minute, then in a very low voice she spoke to him with words that cut into him like a scalpel.

'You mean you knew he was up to something? You knew he was out to get Jack, and you didn't warn me? Well, I hope you're happy now, Kev. Your loyalty to your dad has destroyed the only chance of happiness I've had in years. I just hope you're satisfied.'

Giving him another scalding look, Mum stormed out of the room, leaving him with his thoughts. It was a long time before he moved. He found himself walking into the kitchen to reassure Gareth. He could hear the sound of Mum crying in her room.

# PART TWO

## *Broken Locks*

*The game is about playing football, not punching people.*

West Ham United manager
Harry Redknapp

# One

Kev usually looked forward to the weekend. There were advantages to it being Saturday:

★ It wasn't a school day.

★ You could hang around with your mates and listen to the Everton match on City Sport.

★ You could look forward to Sunday's Junior League game – this week it was Northend United, the first hurdle in the Diamonds' three-match title run-in.

But this Saturday was different. Reasons for it being different:

★ School was sticking its nose into his precious weekend. It was Parents' Evening the following week and, boy, was Mum worked up.

★ The Blues had spent the season flirting with relegation – *again!*

★ Despite facing their three most vital games of the campaign, the Diamonds had definitely gone off the boil.

Oh yes, AND . . .

★ Mum insisted on dragging Kev to town with her.

'But why me?' Kev groaned. 'It's Gareth you're buying trainers for.'

'We've been through this,' Mum answered impatiently. 'No way are you roaming round the estate by yourself while I'm in town. From now on you have to earn your freedom. So if you want to hang around with your mates, do something to deserve it.'

'Such as?'

'We've discussed this, Kev.'

'Oh,' said Kev. 'You mean school.'

'Congratulations,' Mum said sarcastically. 'So I'm not *always* talking to myself.'

'But that's not fair,' said Kev. 'I can't do anything before Parents' Evening.'

'Oh yes, you can.'

'What?'

Mum was rummaging among the junk mail, reading folders and empty cigarette packets on the kitchen surface.

'Has anybody seen my keys?' she asked.

'But what have I got to do?' Kev persisted, ignoring her question. He wished she could forget her stupid keys for a minute.

'That's for you to work out,' said Mum shortly.

'But . . .'

'But nothing, Kevin McGovern. You haven't done a tap in school. Worse still, you've been playing the teachers up.'

She didn't mention keeping Dad's secret about Jack Dougan. Thank heavens for small mercies, thought Kev.

'So,' Mum continued, still searching for her keys, 'work it out for yourself.'

'But what if I can't?'

'Tough,' said Mum. 'You worked out how to be a pain in the neck all by yourself, so work out how to make up for it the same way.'

'But . . .'

'Not another word, Kev. It's a tough old world. Now get yourself sorted. Nobody else can do it for you.'

Kev sighed. She'd been like this all week. The whole thing sucked. Sure, he had to shoulder responsibility for his school report, but she couldn't really blame him for what Dad had done to Dougan. So he'd kept quiet over it. It wasn't a crime, was it? It was Dad who grassed Dougan up. Not him. *Dad.*

'Mum,' shouted Gareth from the living room. 'I've got them.'

He raced excitedly into the kitchen brandishing Mum's keys.

'Good boy,' she said glowingly. 'Where were they?'

'On the telly,' Gareth told her proudly.

'Well, what a helpful little boy,' said Mum. 'There, Kev, that's the sort of thing I was talking about.'

Once her back was turned Kev stuck his tongue out at Gareth, only Gareth didn't just take it. He did it back. Great, thought Kev, now even that little creep's getting one over on me.

'We're catching the one-nine-two,' said Mum, ushering her sons out of the front door. 'We'll get on at the Parade.'

'The Parade?' said Kev. 'Why not at the top of the Avenue?'

'I need some cigarettes,' Mum replied. 'We'll stop off at McGaw's. Any problem with that?'

'Yes,' said Kev. 'A big one, like you killing yourself with those things.'

Gareth looked anxiously at Mum, as if he was expecting her to drop stone-dead that very minute.

'When you start behaving at school,' Mum snapped, 'then I might start listening to you. In the meantime don't you dare lecture me.'

Kev took it on the chin. He didn't have much alternative.

'Now,' said Mum, 'let's get a move on. The bus is due in ten minutes.'

Once inside the newsagent's Kev showed Gareth the

new games section in a couple of computer magazines. Meanwhile Mum bought her cigarettes.

'Do you think Mum will let us borrow this out of the video shop?' Gareth asked, pointing to the new *Deathstorm* game.

'It's an adult one,' said Kev. 'I doubt it.'

He just wanted Gareth to shut up. Costello and Brain Damage were hanging round outside, pulling faces at him through the window.

'We've had older ones out before,' Gareth reminded him.

'Yes,' Kev agreed, doing his best to ignore the antics of Costello and Brain Damage. 'But not an eighteen. Besides, that was when I was in Mum's good books. Look, Gareth, if you want us to hire it you'll have to ask her yourself.'

'OK,' said Gareth boldly, 'I'll ask.'

He was on his way over to Mum when something happened to stop all talk of computer games. Mum had been chatting with Mr McGaw when he broke off in mid-sentence.

'Is something wrong?' Mum asked.

Mr McGaw was staring right past her. The moment she turned round, she saw why. So did Kev. Dad had just emerged from the taxi office. Kev's heart turned over. Mum paid for her cigarettes and almost ran from the shop.

'Your change,' said Mr McGaw, recovering himself.

Kev took it and followed Mum. He dreaded to think what was going to happen next.

'Tony!' Mum shouted, advancing on Dad.

He turned slowly.

'You've done some lousy things,' she said, confronting him. 'But what you did to Jack . . .'

'Oh, cut it out, Carol,' Dad interrupted. 'He's a big boy, and he can take care of himself. He knew the score when he started getting on my back. He can't have been stupid enough to expect me to take it lying down. What's the matter, has Plod dumped you already?'

Mum stared at him for a moment, then drew back her hand and slapped Dad across the face. He took it without flinching.

'Tony,' she said. 'You make me sick. Come on, boys.'

The moment the slap landed, Gareth had burst into tears, and had to be dragged wailing to the bus stop. Kev hesitated for a moment.

'Your mother's waiting for you,' said Dad. He was as cold as ice.

Kev was aware of the whole Parade watching the scene: Mr McGaw, Mr Gulaid, Brain Damage and Costello, and a couple of dozen shoppers and shop-keepers. Now Kev knew what people meant when they wanted the ground to swallow them up.


# Two


If Kev was hoping that a night's sleep was going to make him feel better, then he was sorely mistaken. As he trudged up Owen Avenue to pick up Bashir and Jamie, his stomach was griping constantly, and it wasn't because breakfast was just a Nutri-grain bar. For a match as important as the one against Northend United he ought to be fired up. But he wasn't; his mind was too burdened with thoughts of Mum and Dad. He called on Bashir first.

'Nervous?' asked Bashir as he waved goodbye to his mum. His dad was already down at the shop.

'Numb,' said Kev absent-mindedly.

It was exactly the right word. Part of him was burning with the will to win, but only part of him. As for the rest, well, it was dead tissue. Bashir chose not to probe any further. That was his way. He didn't ask anything of his friends, but if they chose to talk he would always be there to listen.

'It's Mum and Dad,' Kev explained. 'They're getting worse.'

Bashir nodded. There wasn't really much he could say.

They were jogging over the bridge by the Territorial Army Centre when they heard familiar voices.

'I don't know where you're off in such a hurry,' said Costello, emerging from the underpass which ran alongside the biscuit factory. 'Anyone would think you had a serious chance of the title.'

He roared with derisive laughter, and was immediately accompanied by Brain Damage, Tez Cronin, Jelly Wobble, Carl Bain and Mattie Hughes.

'I don't know what you're so cocky about,' said Jamie. 'You're only a point ahead of us.'

'Yes, but look at our fixtures,' said Brain Damage. 'You've got Northend, then Longmoor, then us. Three of the top five in the league. Do you know who we've got before we batter you on the last day? Only the bottom two teams. Why don't you face up to the truth, Diamonds? You've got no chance.'

'What do you know, Brain Damage?' snapped Kev. 'You're not a footballer, you're just . . . a waste of flipping space.'

'I'd be wary of shooting your mouth off,' warned

Costello. 'There are six of us and only three of you.'

'So?' Kev retorted. 'Any one of us is worth a dozen of you, you piece of . . .'

'Guv,' hissed Jamie. 'Shouldn't we just get to the game? There's time for this after the match.'

Kev gave Costello and Co a cold stare, then grudgingly followed Jamie and Bashir along the road. Costello's gang followed about ten yards behind.

'Are you crazy?' whispered Jamie. 'You could have got us hammered back there. It's a good job they want to win today just as much as we do.'

'Jamie,' Kev replied. 'You can't run scared all your life. You need to stand up for yourself.'

'I do stand up for myself,' Jamie shot back. 'It's just that some of us know when to bend a bit. It's called common sense.'

Though it was still a five-minute walk to Jacob's Lane playing fields, Kev and Jamie didn't exchange another word. Their annoyance with each other fairly crackled through the air. Bashir didn't try to patch things up either. He was too busy trying to blot out the chorus of insults from Costello and Co which grew as they were joined by their new striker, a lad by the unfortunate name of Wayne Bowe. The atmosphere in the dressing room wasn't much better. It was like the Warbreck game. The Diamonds' sense of purpose had gone. When he had joined the team eighteen months earlier Kev had given a bunch of no-hopers a vision. It had led them to victory in the Challenge Cup. But now that he was sinking under the weight of his own problems, they were sinking with him.

'What gives?' asked Ratso, the last to arrive. 'Somebody died or something?'

'No,' said John. 'But it can be arranged.'

'Lighten up, will you?' said Ratso. 'After today we could be just two games away from the championship.'

'Yes,' said John. 'Or further away than ever.'

Kev glanced across at Ratso. It was a speech he ought to be giving.

'Ratso's right,' he said, doing his best to blot out thoughts of Mum and Dad. 'This is a big game for us, lads. Losing last week basically put Northend out of the hunt, but they can still hurt us. They've beaten us before, remember. We can't afford to play like we did last week.'

Suddenly he was smiling. *I never go under. I always come through.*

'Northend are nearly good enough to be title contenders themselves. On their day they can give anybody a run for their money.' Kev let this idea sink in, then hit the Diamonds with the punch-line. 'Only we're better. You know it and I know it. We tackle harder, break quicker and take our chances better than any team in the league. We put eleven past Ajax Aintree in our two meetings and they're lying second. There's only one team who can stop us taking the championship, and that's ourselves.'

Ant finished lacing his boots.

'Come again?'

'Look at the games we've lost,' said Kev. 'Every single defeat was self-inflicted, especially when Northend beat us in the winter. We've got the talent. The question is, have we got the bottle?'

Kev noticed Jamie looking at him. But before Jamie could say anything, Ronnie appeared to give his team talk. It wasn't a patch on Kev's. Ronnie told them what they already knew, but Kev was capable of getting them thinking.

'Jimmy, *Jimmy*, you meff,' Kev bawled. 'You've got to get closer to your man. That lad's quick. You can't afford to let him get a run at you.'

Jimmy nodded, but did little about it. He clearly thought he had the pace to see off the danger, and he wasn't going to take advice in that tone of voice.

'Might as well talk to myself,' Kev grumbled as he set off up the pitch.

The confidence he had felt in the dressing room was ebbing. For starters, the Diamonds had almost conceded within five minutes. They still weren't firing on all cylinders. It was one thing to talk the good fight, it was quite another to actually fight it. Then there was the little matter of the Liver Bird playing on the adjacent pitch. They'd scored within two minutes and were already two-nil up.

Costello hadn't wasted any time conveying the news. He looked like a cat who'd swallowed the canary.

'Chris,'. Kev called, making a run into open space. 'Pass it.'

But the ball took a bad bobble and Chris miscued it straight to the Northend left-winger. He controlled it with his instep and set off down the touch-line. He looked to have the beating of Jimmy, but Chris got across to make up for his mistake.

'What did I say, Jimmy? Get tighter on him. You deaf, or what?'

Jimmy raised his eyes.

'Are you listening to me?' Kev asked.

'Do I have much choice?' sighed Jimmy.

'What do I have to do to get through to him?' Kev wondered out loud.

'Talking to him properly might help,' said Jamie.

'This is football,' scoffed Kev. 'Not rotten croquet.'

'Come off it, Kev,' said Jamie. 'We all know how much you want to win, but you're biting everybody's head off.'

'All I want,' Kev told his friend, 'is a bit of effort. Is that too much to ask?'

Jamie turned away. Kev was obviously not in the mood to listen.

'Come on, lads,' Kev shouted. 'Let's get our passing game going.'

But it was Northend who got their passing game going. A neat triangle of passes put their left-winger away on the edge of the penalty area. Realizing too late that Kev had been right about his marking, Jimmy tried to muscle his man off the ball. He did, but gave away a penalty in the process.

'Don't say it,' a crestfallen Jimmy told Kev.

Kev saw Jamie looking at him.

'Forget it,' Kev said, taking the unspoken advice. 'No use crying over spilt milk.'

Northend converted the spot-kick to go one-nil up, but that wasn't the worst of it. With their confidence sky-high, Northend started playing slick, first-touch football, carving the Diamonds open at least four times. The Diamonds were raising the game, but still not to the height of Northend's impressive performance. Fortunately Daz was playing a blinder in goal, stopping a point-blank shot with his feet and tipping a rasping fifteen-yarder over with his fingertips. The last fifteen minutes of the first half was as searching a test as the Diamonds had had all season. In the event, they went in still only one goal adrift. They were lucky and they knew it.

# Three

The Diamonds listened to Ronnie's half-time talk in silence. Their body language said it all. Everybody was sitting, some with their arms on their knees and heads drooping. Ratso had already relayed the other half-times. Longmoor, Ajax and the Liver Bird were all leading. Good news was in short supply. Just to make things worse, one of the Diamonds' former players, Dave Lafferty, had come along to see how his old mates were doing. Dave had been their star striker until Everton snapped him up for their School of Excellence. It was the first time Kev had seen him in weeks and his timing couldn't have been worse.

'I'll keep this short,' said Ronnie. He was rubbing his eyes wearily after coming straight from another night shift at the fire station. 'That was rubbish. You know it, I know it. The marking was slack, the movement poor and the passing . . . Well, I don't remember seeing much, really. On the plus side, you can't play that badly again in the second half. Davey here must be cringing at the first-half display.'

Dave gave an embarrassed smile.

'It's simple, lads,' Ronnie concluded. 'Do you want this title or not?'

The manager ran his eyes over his dispirited troops. They did, but they'd dug themselves a hole and it was hard to climb out. Poor play can be a habit that's hard to break.

'Anyway, you know what you've got to do.'

By the tone of his voice, Ronnie had half given up too, but he did manage an appeal to his captain.

'You're the one who can get them moving, Kev. What about it?'

'I'm trying,' Kev replied.

'You sure about that?'

'Meaning?'

'You've been very up and down just lately. What do they call it, yes, manic-depressive. One minute you're drifting out of the game completely, the next you're your old self, battling for every ball. Which is it to be, Kev?'

Kev saw the Liver Bird taking the field on Pitch Five. Their swift, confident stride was in sharp contrast to the way the Diamonds had returned.

'I'll try to get them going,' he said, fairly downbeat.

'What's the matter, Guv?' asked Dave. 'This isn't the old Guv'nor.'

'Dunno,' Kev replied. 'Anyway, how's things going for you?'

'Good,' said Dave. 'I'm loving it. One of the scouts keeps threatening to take a look at my old team.' He nodded in the direction of his former team-mates. 'Mind you, I'm glad he didn't come today.'

That did it. By the time Kev left Dave he was punching his sides, quietly summoning every ounce of determination. He was going to wipe the smile off Costello's face. His life might be going down the tubes, but the Diamonds weren't about to follow.

'Jamie,' he said. 'Sorry about before. Listen, the service from midfield has been so weak you've had to come infield to get the ball. Forget tracking back, just stay out wide on the right. Bashir, same for you, we've got to get behind them.' He strode forward flinging instructions in all directions. 'John, Ratso, get the ball out to the flanks whenever you can. Liam, Conor, don't go searching for the ball. Just make your runs and rely on us to get it through to you.'

In the corner of his eye, Kev glimpsed Ronnie passing a comment to his subs. The manager liked what he saw. So did Dave Lafferty. He gave Kev the thumbs up.

'OK lads,' Kev said. 'We made a show of ourselves in the first half. Time to put on the style.'

The first ten minutes' play didn't see any miracles from the Diamonds. Passes still went astray and there were misunderstandings, but something had changed. The wingers might not have broken down the Northend defence, but at least they were in the game. Just as important, the midfield trio of John, Ratso and Kev were playing as a unit, with Kev providing the inspiration.

'This is better, Guv,' said Jamie. 'We're the ones calling the shots.'

'Yes,' Kev agreed. 'And it's about time.'

It was their partnership that opened Northend up for the first time that morning. Kev spotted Jamie dropping off his marker and flighted the ball skilfully into the space in front of him. Seizing the chance, Jamie powered to the bye-line and cut the ball back towards the penalty spot, where Conor was waiting. It was the first chance to come his way and it showed. He rushed his shot and actually struck the ball with his shin. It didn't make any difference. The ball scudded into the net past the keeper's despairing reach.

One-one.

'Right lads,' Kev urged. 'We're on level terms, now let's turn up the heat.'

Even the non-believers like John O'Hara started to show a new confidence in their play. Bashir and Jamie were ready to put Northend to the sword, raiding down the flanks at will. The crosses were coming in from all angles and Liam and Conor both had chances to put the Diamonds ahead.

'Don't panic,' Kev told his troops. 'There's plenty of time on the clock. We're pressing all the right buttons. Just keep feeding it out wide. They've no answer to Bash and Jamie.'

He was proved right within a minute. It was Bashir who did the damage this time, squeezing between two defenders and back-heeling it to the unmarked Kev. Kev dribbled the ball outside the keeper, then bent his foot round it and poked it goalwards.

Two-one.

The Diamonds were almost caught coming forward when one of the Northend strikers broke clear. Fortunately for the Diamonds, Daz was up to the task and smothered the shot.

'That was a let-off,' Kev declared. 'We still need another goal to kill the game off.'

With five minutes to go, it was Kev himself who laid on the decisive third goal. Pulling wide of the advancing Bashir, he rose to nod down the winger's flick. To his delight, Liam was on it in a flash and stroked it beautifully inside the left-hand post.

Three-one.

'Game, set and match, Guv,' chuckled Ratso.

Kev slapped him on the back and winked at Dave standing on the touch-line. 'Let's just hope somebody's dropped a point, eh, Rats. We've done our bit.'

But as he turned ready for the re-start, the blood drained from Kev's face.

'Guv,' Ratso asked. 'What's wrong?'

Kev didn't reply. Instead he started walking towards the touch-line.

'Kevin?' Ronnie asked. 'Where are you going?'

'Something's wrong,' Kev replied. 'Give me a minute, will you, Ron?'

The cause of Kev's sudden departure soon became obvious to the rest of the team. Mum was heading straight for him, dragging Gareth along beside her.

'Mum,' Kev asked, approaching the touch-line. 'What's the matter?'

'I thought you'd better know,' she told him. 'Your dad's at Harbour Lane police station. He's been arrested.'

# Four

A few minutes later Kev, Mum and Gareth were hurrying up Jacob's Lane, hoping to flag down a taxi. The final whistle was sounding all over the playing fields. Kev hoped the Diamonds hadn't been stupid enough to throw away a two-goal lead.

'Typical,' said Mum. 'There's never a taxi about when you need one.'

Two black cabs had passed but both had fares already.

'But what happened?' Kev asked. 'What's Dad been arrested for?'

'I don't know much more than you.' Mum replied. 'I got a phone call about half an hour after you left for your match. The police raided his flat at seven o'clock this morning. Broke down the door and everything.'

'So where are we going now?'

'Your nan's.'

Kev bit his lip. This had to be serious. Mum hadn't so

much as spoken to Nan McGovern in five years. He found himself staring at Mum.

'What's the matter?' she asked.

'You, I didn't think . . .'

'He's the father of my kids,' Mum said sharply. 'I can't say it's something I'm too happy about, but it's a fact. But don't go reading anything else into this, Kev. If your dad and I weren't finished when he walked out on us, we certainly are now, after what he's done.'

Kev nodded grimly. Dad's flat raided. So it had happened. They'd finally got him. Kev didn't know much about what had happened, but of one thing he was certain. If it wasn't all Dougan's doing then he'd definitely had a part to play in it.

'Mum, Mum,' shouted Gareth suddenly. 'Here's one, and his light's on.'

Mum hailed the taxi and bundled the boys in.

'Appleton Hey,' she told the driver. 'Number seven.'

As the taxi pulled away, Kev could see the teams leaving the playing field. He scanned the stream of boys for signs of the Diamonds. Eventually he spotted Jamie and Bashir chatting to Dave Lafferty. He tried to read the result from the way they were acting but they were deadpan. He would just have to stew.

'Was anyone else picked up?' Kev asked, turning his mind once more to Dad's arrest. He was thinking about Lee Ramage. Wouldn't it be just typical if Dad got banged up and Brain Damage's older, more disgusting brother got off scot-free?

Mum glared at him. 'Keep your voice down,' she hissed, nodding in the direction of the driver. 'I don't want everyone knowing our business.'

'Which way do you want me to go?' the driver asked. 'The Drive or the Parade?'

'I don't think it makes much odds,' said Mum.

'I'll take the Parade then,' said the driver. 'Cut out the traffic lights.'

As they turned into the Parade, Kev got his answer about other arrests. There was a police van and a patrol car parked outside Ramage Taxis. Two uniformed policemen were standing in the doorway, quizzing Ramage's drivers. Two others – CID, Kev guessed – were talking to Mr McGaw outside his shop.

'They must have got Lee Ramage, too,' said Kev.

Mum nodded.

'What a mess,' she murmured. 'I warned Tony. This was bound to happen sooner or later.'

Kev hesitated for a moment, then asked the obvious question. 'Mum,' he said. 'This doesn't have anything to do with Jack Dougan, does it?'

Mum stared at him. 'What do you mean? . . . Oh, I get it, you really think that Jack and I sat plotting how to get your dad locked up. Well, sorry, Kev, but we had better things to do than worry about Tony. Jack didn't talk about his job, and I kept your dad out of the conversation. Besides, Jack's been moved. Even if he was involved in planning this raid, he's got no involvement now.'

Kev wondered whether Mum was telling the truth. That's the trouble with people, he thought, you rely on them but there's no way you can ever really know what's going on in their heads. The taxi pulled up in front of a neat house facing a row of dilapidated-looking tower blocks.

'It's been painted since we came last,' Kev said.

Mum ignored the comment. She obviously took it as a criticism. Come to think of it, Kev thought, that's how it was meant. She never lets me come.

Nan met them at the front door.

'Carol,' she said frostily. 'You came then.'

'Yes,' said Mum. 'I came.'

Her reply was equally sub-zero.

Nan led the way into the living room.

'Any news yet?' asked Mum.

'Yes,' Nan replied. 'My Harry's stood bail for Tony. He's got to report back to the police station in a few weeks.'

'What does that mean?' Kev asked anxiously.

'It means,' Mum replied, 'that your dad will have to wait to see if they're going to charge him.'

Kev's heart was thudding against his ribs. Was this it, was he really going down this time? Chris's dad was in prison and Kev knew what it had done to him.

'Harry's giving him a lift back,' said Nan.

'How is Harry?' asked Mum. 'How's his angina?'

'Much the same,' said Nan. 'And no better for all this. Thanks for asking, all the same.'

Kev felt uncomfortable. Mum didn't really care how his grandad was and Nan wasn't really thanking her for her interest.

'Now boys,' said Nan, 'would you like a drink and some biscuits?'

'Not for me,' said Kev.

'What about you, Gareth?' asked Nan. 'I've got Kit Kats in the cupboard.'

Gareth looked at Mum.

'Can I?'

Mum nodded.

'Did you hear how the old trout talked to me?' Mum seethed the moment Nan was out of the room. 'She acts like it's my fault Tony got arrested. That's rich coming from her. She's the one who brought him up.'

Kev had heard that one before: I blame it on the parents. It had been said about him often enough.

'Cool it, Mum,' hissed Kev, nodding in Gareth's direction.

Gareth looked from Mum to Kev, trying to make sense of the morning's events.

'It's all right, Gareth,' Mum said soothingly. 'Grown-up stuff.'

'Yeah, don't worry about it,' Kev advised. 'Just eat your Kit Kat.'

And when Nan returned that's precisely what Gareth did.

'Just a minute,' Nan said, hurrying to the front window. That sounds like Harry's car now. Yes, they're here.'

Dad was first to appear.

'Carol,' he said gruffly. 'What are you doing here?'

'I just wanted to see you were all right,' said Mum. 'Besides, the boys would have worried.'

Gareth looked up. Worry about what?

'And you?' Dad asked acidly. 'Were you worried, my darling wife? Oh no, I forgot. It was your boyfriend who planned this little wheeze in the first place.'

Mum glanced at Kev and Gareth.

'Tony,' she said. 'Not here.'

'No,' said Dad hotly. 'Not in front of the kids.'

'So what's going to happen?' asked Nan, keen to head off a row.

'I don't know,' Dad replied. 'They'll consider if they've got enough evidence for a case against us.'

'And have they?' asked Mum. 'We saw them raiding the taxi office on the way up.'

Dad waved his hand dismissively. 'Got something on me, Teflon Tony? Behave, girl.'

Mum handed Gareth his coat.

'Well then,' she said. 'If you're OK, we'll be off.'

'Of course I'm OK,' said Dad. 'You can tell that to lover boy.' A mischievous smile crossed his lips. 'Oh no, I forgot, he's gone, hasn't he?'

Kev's heart sank. Dad was determined to pick a fight.

'Tony,' Mum said. 'When you talk to me like that, I don't know why I stayed with you so long.'

As Kev followed Mum to the front door, Nan prompted Dad: 'Go and say goodbye. They *are* your kids, for goodness' sake.'

Mum and Gareth were already at the front gate, but Kev had hung back to speak to Dad. He just wanted Dad to tell him there was nothing to worry about, that it was all a storm in a teacup. A moment later he wished he hadn't.

'Nice friends you've got, Kev,' said Dad. 'I've warned you off that Gulaid kid. Now look what's happened. His old man's blown me and Lee up to the coppers.'

'I've told you before,' Kev protested. 'You're barking up the wrong tree. Mr Gulaid wouldn't do that.'

'Then who else did it?' Dad demanded. 'Acting on information received, that's what the coppers said. Now whose information would that be, I wonder?'

'It wasn't Mr Gulaid,' Kev insisted.

'I hope not,' said Dad, 'because if it was . . .' He slammed a fist into his palm. 'If it was I wouldn't like to be in his shoes.'

# Five

*What was it Ronnie called me? Oh yes, a manic depressive. Well, is it any wonder? At half past eleven this morning I was on top of the world. I'd just about picked myself up and led the team to victory after falling behind early on (Yes, we did win. Jamie phoned me when I got in), then Dad goes and gets himself arrested and everything blows up in my face. I don't seem to be in control of anything any more. The moment the slightest little thing goes right for me and I feel like smiling, the world falls right in on me again. And have I done one rotten thing to deserve it? No way. I mean, seeing Dave Lafferty reminded me what I want out of life, a chance at the big time. So why does this keep happening to me? I'll tell you why. In the lottery of life I happened to get myself the wrong parents. Wonderful, I really had a hand in that, didn't I? Now I'm condemned to sit out the final weeks of the season when I should be really focused, with my guts churning away inside me, wondering whether Dad's going to end up in Walton nick. Great life, isn't it? But if anybody thinks I'm about to throw in the towel, they can think again. We've still got our eyes on the prize. We can still win something this season – even if it is by the skin of our teeth.*

# Six

Kev could hardly believe it. It was Tuesday evening before he looked properly at the league table Ratso had handed him at training. A whole day when thoughts of Mum and Dad, of police raids and the forthcoming Parents' Evening had crowded football right out of his mind. The funny thing was, no matter how tough the going got, Kev never quite gave in to the pressure. He wasn't like John or Jamie. He never seemed to go on a prolonged downer. There was always part of him that wanted to pop up and spit the world in the eye. What was he, the original rubber man? Hit him and he bounces back, beat him and he just goes boing!

'Can I have another half an hour up?' Gareth asked, slopping across the room in his Godzilla dressing gown and his Everton slippers.

Kev looked up from the grubby piece of notepaper.

'I don't know,' he said. 'What's the time?'

Gareth squinted at the wall clock. 'The long hand's . . .'

'Oh, don't they teach you the time at school?' Kev snapped, sounding just like Mum. 'It's half past seven.'

'So can I have time up?'

Kev was quite enjoying this. Suddenly he had the awesome power of telling his kid brother when to go to bed. It had been quite a turn-up, Mum allowing him to baby-sit while she went to Parents' Evening. It had taken a good hour of soul-searching before she finally let him, of course, with the usual Pros and Cons debate.

*Pros*:-

Gives our Kev a chance to show how responsible he is.

Means I don't have to ask Cheryl to come over.

*Cons*:-

This is Kev we're talking about!

'Kev, can I?' whined Gareth, unable to cope with the tension.

'Go on, then,' said Kev.

'Yiss!'

'But you've got to stay in the living room with your toys. No pestering me, right.'

'Anything, Kev, anything you say.'

Kev smiled as Gareth scampered away with his moon-station set. At least he was a hero in somebody's eyes. As the smile faded from his lips, Kev turned back to the league table. It made interesting reading. Longmoor and Ajax had both ended up dropping points, each drawing with lowly opposition.

'Pressure showing, eh?' Kev said gloatingly.

With the Liver Bird and the Diamonds winning their matches, the league leaders were neck and neck. The table read:

|  | Pl | W | D | L | Pts |
|---|---|---|---|---|---|
| Longmoor Celtic | 20 | 12 | 5 | 3 | 41 |
| Ajax Aintree | 20 | 11 | 7 | 2 | 40 |
| Liver Bird | 20 | 12 | 4 | 4 | 40 |
| Rough Diamonds | 20 | 12 | 3 | 5 | 39 |

'It's in our hands,' Kev told himself. 'All we have to do is beat Longmoor and scummy Liver Bird, then if Ajax drop points we're there.'

Kev didn't talk about the Liver Bird any more. For the last week they were just *The Garbage,* or *The Scum.*

The feeling was mutual. Hostility at school was fast reaching boiling point and only Kev's promise to Mum to keep out of trouble was preventing a war. A few minutes later Kev consulted the clock.

'A quarter to eight,' he said out loud. 'She should be home any time.'

Hearing a noise at the back door, Kev turned round expecting to see Mum walking in. But it was Bashir.

'Guv,' he said, looking round furtively. 'Can I come in?'

Bashir looked troubled.

'Don't worry about Mum, Bash, she's out. Something up?'

'You could say that. Kev, I don't know how to say this.'

Kev's heart thumped. This had to be bad news.

'Then just say it.'

Bashir sat down opposite Kev.

'I think he's at it again.'

It didn't take a genius to work out who *he* was.

'Somebody had a go at the shop's security shutters last night. They broke a couple of locks.'

'And you think it's my dad?'

Bashir lowered his eyes.

'Him and Ramage. Who else could it be?'

Kev didn't even argue. He was past that. He'd been defending Dad for nearly two years, ever since he returned to the Diamond. And every single, lousy time, Dad had let him down. Kev just couldn't do it any more.

'Is there any damage?'

He was thinking *fire damage*. That was Dad's trade-mark, after all.

'No,' Bashir replied. 'Somebody must have disturbed them before they got in. My dad's worried though. He's trying to get the other shopkeepers to start a Shop Watch.'

'Come again?'

'They take it in turns to keep an eye on each other's shops. Night patrols, that sort of thing. Everybody's a bit scared though. Mr McGaw says it's the police's job.'

'And your dad doesn't agree?'

'This happened *after* the police raid,' Bashir reminded him. 'Your dad and Ramage seem to be above the law. Nobody believes they'll go down.'

For a moment Kev felt angry. Who did Bashir think he was talking to? OK, so Dad was a disgrace, but he was still his dad.

'I see your point,' Kev muttered grudgingly.

He was silent for a moment or two, mulling Bashir's information. Eventually he spoke.

'What do you expect me to do, Bash? Me and Dad hardly talk.'

'I know. We don't blame you. But if you hear anything . . .'

His voice trailed off.

'I wish there was something I could do,' Kev told him. 'Dad doesn't listen to me. He doesn't tell me anything either.'

'I know,' said Bashir, getting up. 'I just wanted to talk, I suppose. It's terrible at home. Dad's really angry, but Mum's frightened. I just wish there was something I could do.'

'Me too, Bash,' said Kev. 'Me too.'

Bashir gave a half-smile, then glanced at the league table.

'We're in with a chance, aren't we?'

Kev smiled.

'So long as we're alive and kicking,' he said. 'There's always a chance.'

Mum didn't get in until nearly half past nine. Kev had finally got Gareth up to bed at ten to, and that was a struggle.

'You're late,' said Kev, anxiously. He was trying to read her thoughts from the expression on her face. It wasn't much use. She just looked wet from the evening showers.

'A lot to talk about,' said Mum, unzipping her jacket and shaking off the raindrops. 'Make me a coffee please, love.'

Kev hurried to the kettle. At least she was still talking to him.

'So how did it go?' he asked.

Mum tossed an olive green book on to the kitchen surface.

'Mr Graham wants me to do this with you.'

Kev looked at the book. He'd seen them before. Chris Power had had one for a while. Brain Damage had gone through three! 'So he's put me on report.'

'Yes. Your teachers keep a daily log of your behaviour and progress and I sign it every evening. I'll go in at the end of term to discuss the results with Mr Graham.'

'Anything else?' asked Kev.

'Only that you're a bright lad,' said Mum.

Kev shook his head. Was there something wrong with his hearing?

'Come again?'

'Your test results are really good,' Mum explained. 'Especially considering you hardly ever do any work. I suppose you know that Peter's going into the top set next year.'

'Peter?' asked Kev, wondering what this had to do with anything. 'Oh, you mean Ratso. Yeah, he's dead clever.'

'The thing is,' Mum went on, 'Mr Graham says you could join him, as long as you do some work between now and the end of term.'

'Me?' said Kev. 'In with the swots? Behave.'

'No, Kev,' said Mum reaching for her cigarettes.

'You behave. Mr Graham says that if you can present your teachers with some decent written work to back up your test scores, you could move up a set. It seems you've got the intelligence. You just don't try. You don't understand, do you? We're talking about your future.'

Kev didn't know what to say. Him, a brainbox? He'd never hear the end of it from the lads, or from Brain Damage and Costello. But there was a tiny part of him that was pleased. So he wasn't just good at football. He'd always been in too much trouble at school to get good marks. But now they reckoned he had a brain all of a sudden. Wonders would never cease!

'Did Gareth go up all right?' Mum asked, sipping her coffee.

'Oh yes,' Kev answered, lying through his teeth. 'Eight o'clock on the dot.'

'Well well,' said Mum, permitting herself a smile. 'Clever *and* responsible.'

# Seven

The next day was an unruffled day, almost a perfect one. Encouraged by Mum's positive remarks the previous evening, Kev decided to give *this work lark* a try. In lessons that Friday he came up with three reasons why British navigators criss-crossed the globe, offered an explanation for condensation on the classroom window and correctly worked out the percentage of kids in class with blue eyes. The upshot of this sudden burst of enthusiasm was a trio of narrowly averted heart-attacks as the teachers staggered back in amazement. Ratso and

Chris ribbed him about it all dinnertime. Best of all, Costello and Brain Damage were really quiet. Thoughts of Dad were almost banished.

Almost.

'What's happening with your old man?' Jamie asked out of the blue on the way home.

Kev realized he must have reacted badly because Jamie shrank back.

'You know as much as I do,' Kev replied. 'I don't think he's heard from the coppers yet.'

He had to say *I don't think* because Dad had done another of his disappearing acts. He hadn't been in touch at all, even though he was supposed to be taking Kev and Gareth out somewhere the next day.

'I wouldn't worry, Guv,' said Jamie. 'He won't get done.'

'How do you know?'

'Because,' Jamie answered, 'he's Lee Ramage's right-hand man and Ramage always comes up smelling of roses. The coppers have pulled him in loads of times and they've never pinned anything on him.'

Kev pulled a face. 'There's always a first time.'

They took a short cut past the cleansing depot.

'Jamie,' Kev said as they entered the Diamond. 'Did you know somebody tried to get into Mr Gulaid's shop last night?'

'No, it's news to me. It was your dad, you mean?'

'I wouldn't put it past him,' said Kev. 'He's convinced it was Mr Gulaid who blew him and Ramage up to the coppers.'

'He must be mad,' said Jamie. 'I mean, he's in big enough trouble as it is.'

'Tell me about it,' sighed Kev.

They'd reached the bottom of Owen Avenue.

'Do you fancy taking a butchers?' asked Kev.

'What, now?'

'Yes, you ask your mum. Say we're running a message to the Parade.'

Jamie nodded and set off home. 'I'll be back in a minute,' he told Kev.

Kev nodded and walked confidently through the back door.

'What's the matter with you?' asked Mum. She was reading a magazine and smoking.

'Only this,' said Kev, tossing the report book over to her.

'Well done!' exclaimed Mum, taking in the good news at a glance.

'Can I have my pocket money?' asked Kev. 'There's a new Everton poster I want to get.'

'Be my guest,' said Mum cheerfully. 'There's some change on top of the microwave.'

'Mum,' Kev asked as he rummaged in the change, 'has Dad been in touch about tomorrow? He was talking about me stopping over at his flat.'

'No,' said Mum, the smile vanishing from her face. 'And I'm not expecting him to. Are you?'

'Not really,' said Kev, disappointed despite Dad's recent track record. 'I just thought . . .'

'I know, son,' said Mum. 'It's hard, but he's been letting us both down for the last twelve years.'

'There must have been good times,' Kev suggested.

'There were,' Mum agreed. 'At the beginning, and when I gave him a second chance after the first time he cleared off.'

'First time?' asked Kev.

'Oh yes,' Mum explained. 'He's taken off a few times. You were too young to understand. The vanishing acts usually coincided with police interest in what he was doing.'

Kev lowered his eyes. Mention of police interest was still a sore point. Jack Dougan might be absent but he wasn't forgotten.

'Oh,' said Mum. 'Here's Jamie at the door. Is he going with you?'

Kev nodded. 'We won't be long.'

There wasn't much to see at the Gulaids' shop. But that couldn't be said of Ramage's taxi firm. The shutters were firmly locked and there was a hastily scrawled note pasted to the door: *Closed until further notice.*

'It's been like that since the raid,' said somebody behind them.

'Oh hi there, Bashir,' said Kev. 'We came to have a nose at the shop. They didn't do much damage then?'

'Not this time,' said Bashir. 'But Dad thinks they'll come back. He's going to sleep in the shop for a couple of nights, in case they try again.'

'Is that a good idea?' asked Jamie.

'My mum doesn't think so,' Bashir replied. 'She's been pleading with him not to do it. She thinks he might get hurt.'

She's right, thought Kev, but he didn't say it out loud.

'Ready for the Longmoor game?' asked Bashir.

'Are you kidding?' said Kev. 'Raring to go, Bash, raring to go.'

'You're in a good mood,' said Bashir.

Kev wondered whether he'd overdone the enthusiasm bit. After all, Bashir was genuinely worried about the threats to his dad.

'Haven't you heard about the new Guv'nor?' asked Jamie, with a mischievous glint in his eye. 'Only top of the class.'

'What, *you*?' asked Bashir disbelievingly. 'I thought you hated school.'

'Jamie's exaggerating,' Kev told him. 'Mum read the riot act so I had to show willing.'

Bashir was about to say something else when his eyes widened. 'Uh oh.'

Kev and Jamie turned round. Lee Ramage's white BMW was cruising slowly down the Parade.

'It's the heavy mob,' murmured Jamie.

Kev's throat tightened. As usual Dad was at the wheel. As the car slowed outside his shop, Mr Gulaid appeared at the door.

'What do you want?' he asked.

'Just neighbourly interest,' said Lee Ramage. 'I hear you had a spot of bother.'

'You'd know all about that,' Mr Gulaid answered defiantly.

'What's that supposed to mean?' demanded Ramage.

'As if you didn't know.'

'Be careful what you're saying,' warned Dad.

'I'm not scared of you,' said Mr Gulaid. 'Either of you.'

'Well, you should be,' said Dad, before shifting his attention to Kev. 'I thought I'd told you to be more choosy about your company, son.'

Kev knew this was a challenge. Your friends or your dad. This time, painful as it was, there was only one choice.

'I am choosy,' he replied as forcefully as his cracking voice would allow. 'That's why I'm staying right here.'

Dad gave Kev a long, cold stare, then drove off.

'You were very brave,' said Mr Gulaid, resting a hand on Kev's shoulder.

Kev nodded. He couldn't come up with a reply though. He was too close to tears.

## Eight

*I thought doing the right thing was supposed to make you feel good. It does in the movies. Stand up for your friends and you get the works: full symphony orchestra, heavenly choir, cast of thousands cheering you to the closing credits. Not me, I just get a rotten lump in the throat and no day out with Dad. Something tells me this really is the final break with him. He wanted to know where I stood and I told him. Mr Gulaid was right: I was brave. My legs were shaking like mad and I was nearly crying, but I still plucked up the courage to look Dad in the eye and tell him where to get off. The only trouble is, I cut part of my heart out doing it. Worse still, I'm not even that convinced it did any good. Let's face it, a man who can walk out on his wife and kids for four whole years is hardly going to see the light just because I tell him I think what he's doing is wrong. Dad and Ramage are still gunning for the people who informed the police and the Gulaids are still in the frame. This isn't over just because I made my stand, not by a long chalk.*

## Nine

It was half past eleven the following morning before Kev finally gave up on his dad. He wouldn't be staying over at his flat this week, or ever. Yes, he knew in his heart of hearts that the break was final and yes, he knew there was no chance of Dad turning up to keep his appointment. It didn't stop him pacing the living-room floor and flying to the front window every time a car pulled up.

'You'd better face it, Kev,' Mum said, looking up from the TV. 'He isn't coming. You may as well go to New Brighton with your mates.'

Kev nodded and ran upstairs to get the ball of string and his Saveaway ticket from his bedside table. Jamie, Chris and Bashir were going crab-fishing. They were meeting at Rice Lane station at noon.

'Kev,' Mum called as he searched frantically for any loose change in the three pairs of jogging pants on his bedroom floor. 'It's nearly twenty to.'

'I know,' Kev shouted back. 'I need another fifty pence for the chippy.'

'Here,' said Mum. 'I'll advance you next week's pocket money. Now get a move on.'

Kev thundered downstairs, snatched the money gratefully and flew to the door.

'Thanks would be nice,' Mum reminded him.

'Oh yes, thanks,' Kev panted before dashing off down the street, slamming the door behind him.

He checked his watch as he passed the site where a supermarket was being built opposite Cropper Lane school. Ten to. He was cutting it fine. Dodging the traffic on Hornby Road, he caught sight of Chris, Jamie and Bashir at the top of the steps that led down to the platform. Chris was looking at his watch. A few seconds later Kev heard the loud rumble of the train arriving.

'Hang on, lads,' he shouted.

But they hadn't heard him. They were running down the steps.

'Come on, Kev,' he told himself. 'You can do it.'

He flew down the steps and burst through the train doors just as they closed. Made it!

'Impressive entrance,' chuckled Jamie as Kev dropped, breathing heavily, on to the seat next to him.

'I was waiting for my dad,' he explained.

His mates swopped glances.

'I know, I know,' said Kev. 'I'm living in a dream world. Got all the stuff?' he asked, changing the subject.

Bashir pulled two empty plastic ice-cream containers from a holdall. Chris produced a ball of string from his jacket. Jamie opened a carrier bag to reveal half a dozen lumps of whitish-pink offcuts of meat.

'Yeuch, gross,' said Chris.

'It'll do the job,' said Kev. 'We'll have those crabs clinging to it like . . . crabs clinging to meat.'

Everybody laughed.

'Hang on,' said Jamie. 'Here comes the ticket inspector.'

The boys waved their tickets. The inspector looked suspiciously at the bag of meat.

'It's his cousin,' Kev quipped. 'He was getting on our nerves.'

'Yes,' said Chris. 'We dismembered him this morning.'

'Kids,' snorted the inspector. He had the sense of humour of a conger eel.

The boys messed around Moorfields station for a while, running up the down escalator and booting a squashed Coke can around, then caught their connection to New Brighton.

Once out of the station at the other end, they headed for the marine lake where people were already lined up on the side, fishing for crabs.

'This'll do,' said Jamie. 'Let's get started.'

They quickly tied lengths of string to the offcuts of meat and started dangling the bait in the water. Within fifteen minutes they were reeling in dozens of crabs.

'Look at the size of this one,' shouted Bashir, pulling his chunk of meat out of the water. A crab the size of his fist was clinging to the underside.

'Cor,' said Chris, who'd never been to New Brighton before. 'Jaws.'

'Claws, more like,' said Kev. 'How many's that?'

Jamie inspected the plastic tubs which were now a mass of claws and crusty legs.

'Thirty-five, I think,' said Bashir.

'No,' said Chris, pulling on his string. 'Thirty-six.'

'There's two of them,' Kev laughed. 'Thirty-seven.'

And on they went until gone half past two.

'Ninety-nine,' declared Bashir. 'Let's make it a round hundred then get some dinner. I'm starving.'

Chris nodded. 'Me too.'

'We could try one of these,' said Kev, lifting a dark brown crab from the tub. He looked at it for a moment then grimaced. 'Maybe not.'

The hundred came up two minutes later. Kev noticed two girls watching them.

'Want to take over?' he asked. 'We're going.'

The girls nodded and took the strings.

'You old romantic,' Jamie teased. 'Most girls get roses.'

'And you'll get a thick ear if you don't shut up,' Kev retorted.

After refuelling on fish, chips and peas and Dr Pepper, the boys headed home.

'That was excellent,' said Chris. 'When can we go again?'

'Any time you want,' said Kev. 'Hey, listen to the sound of the train.'

'What are you on about?' asked Jamie.

'It's like a chant,' said Kev. '*We're going to win, we're going to win, we're going to win.*'

'You know what?' Bashir said. 'It does sound like it.'

They they were all chanting it out:

*We're going to win,*
*We're going to win,*
*We're going to WIN.*'

'Win what?' asked an old lady who was sitting across the aisle.

'Our next to last footy match,' Kev explained. 'It's tomorrow. If we win this and one more, we could be champions.'

That set off a chorus of:

'*Champion-es,*
*Champion-es,*
*Oh-ay*
*Oh-ay*
*Oh-ay.*'

'Well, good luck, boys,' said the old lady as she got off.

'Thanks, missus,' said Kev, suddenly full of confidence. 'Only we don't need luck.'

But when they got off the train at Rice Lane, it was back to reality. Brain Damage, Costello and Tez Cronin were riding round on their bikes.

'Heard the news, McGovern?' asked Brain Damage. 'Your dad and our Lee are off the hook.'

Kev's heart missed a beat.

'What do you mean?'

'Lee got the letter this morning. Insufficient evidence to proceed.'

Costello laughed. 'Coppers are pathetic. They couldn't organize a bun fight in a bakery.'

Kev stared back at them. Was this another wind-up?

'You don't look too happy, McGovern,' said Brain Damage.

'Aw, what's the matter?' Costello taunted. 'Not talking to daddums?'

'You won't be talking to anybody if you don't watch your mouth,' Kev warned him.

'Ooh-ooh,' chorused Costello, Brain Damage and Cronin before cycling slowly away.

'Anyway, don't get your knickers in a twist, McGovern,' said Costello. 'You don't want to get all tense before the big game, do you?'

'Get lost,' snapped Kev.

'You against the top team and us against the bottom,' Brain Damage smirked. 'By this time tomorrow you'll be out of the chase.'

'In your dreams, Brain Damage,' shouted Jamie. 'Don't let them get to you, Guv.'

Kev rolled his eyes. 'They don't bother me.'

But they did. Not about the match. Kev was feeling upbeat. It was Dad and Lee Ramage.

Now the police were off their back, they were free to do their worst.

# PART THREE

# *Rude Shocks*

*The ref told me if I made the save we'd win. I hadn't made a save all game so I thought this would be a good time.*

Sasa Ilic of Charlton Athletic

# One

True to his word, Ratso was sticking to the anthem he had chosen right to the bitter end. As the Diamonds took to the field on the penultimate Sunday of the season 'The Final Countdown' was blaring out of his ghetto blaster.

'Inspirational, eh?' he said with a wink to Kev.

'Let's hope so,' said Kev.

For the second week running, the Diamonds' match was taking place on the adjacent pitch to the Liver Bird game. Costello and Brain Damage acknowledged Kev by giving him the thumbs down.

'Longmoor will murder you, McGovern.'

'No chance,' said Kev, but he wasn't as confident as he sounded. While his team faced last year's champions and the leading side again this season, the Liver Bird had only to beat second-to-bottom Warbreck.

'We'll see,' said Costello, joining the rest of his team. 'We'll see.'

Kev surveyed Longmoor as they had a pre-match kick-about. Kitted out in their green and white hooped jerseys and white shorts, they looked formidable. Kev registered their danger men. Up front they had Bobby Sutton and Phil Gallacher, both scorers when they defeated the Diamonds four-three on the opening day of the season. They had another potential match winner in their skipper Gerry Darke. He had also scored in their previous encounter. The referee whistled and called the two captains over.

'Call,' he told them.

'Heads,' said Kev.

It was tails.

'We'll kick off,' said Gerry Darke.

Both teams were cagey in the opening stages. Long-moor wanted maximum points, but a draw wouldn't be a disaster for them. Not so the Diamonds. Two points behind, they were desperate to win.

As the players settled into their routines, it was Longmoor who got their game going first, probing the Diamonds' defence with a couple of promising moves.

'Keep it tight,' Kev told his defenders. 'Don't hang on to the ball. If in doubt, launch it.'

He was becoming anxious about some jittery play by the Diamonds' central defenders, Gord and Ant. They seemed tense and were committing themselves to the tackle too early. It was especially true of Ant. Whenever he was having a poor game, he would take it out on his team-mates.

'Cover me, will you, Gord?' he barked, after conceding a corner.

'Cover you?' Gord replied. 'You should have cleared that for a throw-in when you had the chance. Don't go blaming me for your mistakes.'

'Cut it out,' Kev ordered. 'Don't let Longmoor see us arguing among ourselves.'

The corner was a poor one and sailed out of play past the far post.

'Danger over,' said Kev. 'Now stop squabbling and play for each other.'

He was just trotting back upfield when he heard a roar from the pitch where the Liver Bird were playing. They'd gone one-nil up.

'I suppose you heard,' said Jamie.

Kev nodded.

'It ought to be an incentive to our lads to get their game going,' he said hopefully.

Unfortunately, it didn't work like that. The central defence partnership of Ant and Gord was still creaking and ten minutes into the first half Ant made a dreadful mistake in front of goal. Gathering a hopeful pass by Longmoor skipper Gerry Darke, he looked for options.

Ignoring Gord to his right, Ant tried an ambitious pass to Bashir on the left. It fell short and gave Longmoor possession in a dangerous position. Mark Ridley whipped in a first-time cross right to the head of Longmoor's top scorer Bobby Sutton. He made no mistake, heading strongly into the roof of the net.

One-nil to Longmoor.

As Daz retrieved the ball from the back of his net, the news got even worse. The Liver Bird had gone two-nil up.

'Don't worry, Diamonds,' Costello taunted. 'There's time for you to lose by an even bigger margin.'

Kev was livid at the turn of events and started tackling with a vengeance, single-handedly breaking up the pattern of Longmoor's midfield play. After a characteristically bruising tackle, he stabbed the ball forward to Conor who had oceans of space. Surprised not to be adjudged offside, the normally composed Conor sliced his shot.

'Sorry,' he grimaced.

But not as sorry as the Diamonds were five minutes later. This time Bobby Sutton turned provider, beating Ant to the ball and setting up Phil Gallacher with an easy chance.

Two-nil to Longmoor.

Kev saw the dejection in Ant's face and looked across at Ronnie.

'He's gone,' Kev shouted. 'Completely lost it. Can we have Chris on?'

Ronnie looked at Ant and nodded. Gerry Darke watched the substitution with satisfaction. A change of personnel so early in the first half was a testament to his side's growing superiority.

'Right, Chris,' said Kev. 'You must have heard what I said to Ant. Nothing fancy. Just close down your man and keep it tight. At two-nil we can still get back into the game. If we concede a third it's goodnight Vienna.'

Chris nodded though he didn't know what Vienna had got to do with anything.

'Come on, Diamonds,' Kev shouted. 'Where's your pride?'

'It's not pride you're missing,' said Gerry Darke. 'It's skill.'

Stung by the remark, Kev stormed through the Longmoor defence and slid a silky pass out to Jamie on the right wing. Beating his man, Jamie struck a blistering shot against the nearside post.

'Unlucky,' said Kev.

It was only their second goal-scoring opportunity, but hopefully a sign of things to come. Unfortunately, over at the Liver Bird game, news was even worse for the Diamonds.

'You won't believe this, Guv,' said Ratso. 'But they've got a penalty.'

Kev watched in anguish as Wayne Bowe ran up to take it. To everyone's amazement, the Liver Bird's star striker skied the ball over the crossbar. The score stayed at two-nil.

'Thank goodness for small mercies,' said Kev, as he tried to rally the Diamonds.

In the last ten minutes of the half, their twin strikers

Liam and Conor came into the game more, bringing three good saves out of the Longmoor keeper.

'More like it,' said Kev encouragingly.

On the stroke of half-time, Kev rose for a corner and headed the ball down strongly. It looked a goal all the way, but Longmoor goalie Jonathan Wright was again up to the task, tipping the ball against the post. Gerry Darke cleared.

'Now it's a match,' Kev announced to his team-mates. 'For the last ten minutes we've been taking the game to them. Another push and we can get a goal back before half-time.'

It wasn't to be, however. Just as a Diamonds' goal looked certain, the referee blew his whistle. Ratso immediately set off across the playing field to get the other half-times. When he returned five minutes later, he had mixed news.

'Liver Bird still two-nil up,' he said. 'If the scores stay this way,. we've blown the championship. It'll be between Longmoor and Costello's outfit.'

'What about Ajax?' asked Kev.

'Two-nil down, just like us,' Ratso reported. 'End of season nerves.'

The very thought of Costello and Brain Damage being in with a shout for the league title made Kev's blood boil.

'We've got to do something,' he said determinedly.

'Sure,' said Ratso. 'But what?'

# Two

The answer was surprisingly obvious and came from Ronnie.

'You've got to play better,' he said.

And that was it, one of the shortest half-time team talks of the season. Five words that put it in a nutshell. The advice was so simple some of the Diamonds started to giggle.

'I don't know what you're laughing at,' Kev interrupted angrily. 'Ronnie's right. We're in this position because we conceded two soft goals.'

Ant lowered his head.

'But I'm not just picking on Ant. We were uncertain in defence and toothless in attack. Look at the chance Conor passed up.' Then just to show he wasn't going to spare anyone, Kev turned his wrath on the midfield as well. 'John and Ratso have hardly been in the game and we've had no support from Jimmy. Where are the overlapping runs, for goodness' sake?'

A few resentful eyes turned in Kev's direction.

'Look,' Kev told them bluntly. 'I'm not picking on anybody in particular.'

'Good job,' grunted big Daz Kemble.

Kev ignored the laughter. 'I'm just telling you that we're not playing our best. We've been playing below par for a while now, but we've got away with it against second-rate opposition. This time we're up against the best. That means we play at the top of our game or we forget the championship.'

'Couldn't have put it better myself,' said Ronnie. 'So that's what we want from you, lads. Total commitment. I don't care if you crawl off this pitch when it's over.

You're going to put every ounce of strength and skill into this second half. If we do our best and still lose – well tough, at least we tried. But if we don't even have a go we'll never forgive ourselves. Come on now, lads, give it your all.'

For five minutes at the start of the second period, Longmoor didn't know what had hit them. In Gerry Darke's case it was literally true. First Kev, then Ratso, and finally John felled him with crunching tackles. The Longmoor playmaker was barely able to raise a canter after that series of challenges. Taking advantage of the lack of direction in the opposition midfield, Kev started spraying out accurate, creative passes. Jamie, Conor and Liam all went close before a cheeky back-heel pulled one back for the Diamonds.

'Inspirational,' said Kev approvingly.

Ratso chuckled.

Only two-one down.

But the Diamonds' dominance was coming to an end. Gerry Darke was too proud to buckle under pressure and started to give as good as he got. Ratso crumpled under one particularly hard tackle.

'It's my knee,' he groaned.

'Can you carry on?' asked Ronnie.

Ratso tried to get up but his face was creased with pain.

'Doubt it.'

Joey Bannen came on for Ratso, but it wasn't like for like. Joey shied away from challenges Ratso would have made without thinking. It was Longmoor's turn to boss the midfield, and only a string of saves by Daz and last-gasp clearances by Gord and Chris kept the Diamonds in the hunt. For five minutes Conor was his side's only representative in the Longmoor half of the field. Everyone else was pulled back behind the ball as the Diamonds tried to weather Longmoor's ferocious attacks. After yet another heroic save, Daz completely lost his temper with his defenders.

'Don't I get any protection?' he stormed, flinging his gloves to the ground. 'Get this stinking ball up their end, will you?'

'Keep your hair on,' said Gord.

It was the wrong thing to say.

'Either you get this ball up the other end,' Daz said, 'or I'll send you home to Mum in half a dozen pieces.'

Kev smiled. Daz had his own line in encouragement. About the same time, the Diamonds received welcome news from the neighbouring pitch. Warbreck had pulled one back.

'Come on, lads,' Kev roared. 'This isn't over yet.'

Beating Gerry Darke to a fifty-fifty ball, Kev exchanged passes with Bashir and drove on through the centre of the park, leaving two Longmoor players in his wake. Just when it looked like he was going all the way by himself he released the ball to Liam, lurking dangerously to his left. Liam had no difficulty slotting the ball home from close range.

Two-two.

As Kev's team-mates mobbed him and Liam, news came of a Warbreck equalizer. Suddenly the whole complexion of the afternoon had changed. Anything was possible now.

'Calm down,' Kev yelled. 'There are still five minutes to go. Keep your concentration.'

He might as well have talked to himself. With the Diamonds still celebrating their equalizer, Bobby Sutton raced down the other end and hammered home the simplest of goals. The Diamonds were behind again, and to a real sucker punch.

Two-three down.

Grinding his teeth in sheer fury, Kev flew at his defenders.

'What did I say? What did I tell you, eh? Concentrate. Keep your minds on the rotten game. So what do you do? Tell me. That's right, you go to sleep. Morons.'

As he concluded his tirade by kicking seven shades of red out of the goalpost, he saw an amused Luke Costello grinning at him.

'You've blown it, McGovern,' he smirked.

Not yet we haven't, Kev told himself. Re-starting the game, Kev took the return ball from Conor and started to work it forward. He managed to put Jamie away and could only watch in dismay as Jamie's shot flew inches past the right-hand upright.

'How long left, Kev?' asked Liam.

'Two minutes, maybe three,' Kev told him.

The Longmoor goal-kick was a poor one and John had no difficulty chesting it down and passing to Bashir. The little winger was fully aware of the urgency of the situation and weaved, jinked and dribbled his way past three defenders before flighting the ball across the goalmouth. Conor dived in and headed straight at the keeper. As the ball bounced out, Liam volleyed it back in only for Gerry Darke to clear off the line. Checking his watch, the ref signalled a corner.

'Last chance,' bawled Kev, his heart beating fit to burst. 'Everybody forward.'

It was all the encouragement Daz needed. The big Diamonds' keeper started his run at the half-way line and was still going when Jamie took the corner kick. Crashing through a forest of players Daz headed powerfully towards the goal only for Gerry Darke to stop the ball on the line for a second time. The whistle was already in the referee's mouth when Kev got on the end of the spinning clearance. Shutting his eyes he swung his boot and hoped for the best.

'Goal!'

The magic word burst through Kev's brain as two Longmoor defenders belatedly flattened him.

'Goal, goal, goal!'

Kev was still eating mud from the defenders' challenge when his own team-mates came piling on top of him.

'What a goal.'

'What a skipper.'

'The Guv'nor!'

Thirty seconds and it was all over. A glorious three-three draw, but was it enough to keep the Diamonds in the hunt? Had the Liver Bird snatched a late winner? Ratso raced off to get the full times.

As he came panting back, the Diamonds waited, completely exhausted by their efforts. Barely able to breathe, Kev was bent double, hands on knees.

'Well?'

'Ajax got beaten,' Ratso informed the team. 'They've lost ground.'

'Stuff Ajax,' said Kev. 'What about the Liver Bird?'

Ratso paused for a second. He'd saved the best till last.

'Ratso,' said Kev. 'Spit it out.'

'They drew,' Ratso yelled. 'Warbreck hung on for a draw.'

As the Diamonds erupted in wild celebration, Ratso sat with a scrap of paper drawing up the league table as it stood with one game to go. It read:

| | Pl | W | D | L | Pts |
|---|---|---|---|---|---|
| Longmoor Celtic | 21 | 12 | 6 | 3 | 42 |
| Liver Bird | 21 | 12 | 5 | 4 | 41 |
| Rough Diamonds | 21 | 12 | 4 | 5 | 40 |
| Ajax Aintree | 21 | 11 | 7 | 3 | 40 |

'Lads, lads,' Ratso shouted, trying to get some attention. 'Do you want to know what it means or not?'

'Go on,' said Kev. 'Let's hear it.'

'As you know, next Sunday we play the Liver Bird . . .'

Hoots and catcalls from the Diamonds.

'But Longmoor play Ajax the same day.'

Roars and laughter.

'And we've got the best goal difference of the lot. So-o . . .'

Ratso's brow was furrowed with concentration.

'If we win against the Liver Bird and Longmoor lose or draw against Ajax, the title's ours.'

No sooner were the words out of Ratso's mouth than he was engulfed by his team-mates. They could hardly wait for the following Sunday.

# Three

Unfortunately for Kev, there was a whole week to go before the big game. Little did he know how many shocks there were in store before that final hurdle. The first came as early as Tuesday afternoon.

'Mum,' he shouted excitedly as he burst into the kitchen. 'Mum, wait till you see the report book. You won't believe . . .'

He was stopped in his tracks by the sight of a man's tan leather jacket hanging from the coat-hooks in the hall.

'What the . . . ?'

At that moment Gareth walked past, heading for the kitchen.

'Hey pipsqueak,' said Kev. 'Whose is this?'

But Kev knew the answer before Gareth so much as said a word.

'It's Jack's,' Gareth said as though he was a regular visitor. Barely able to believe the sudden turn-around, Kev followed his little brother into the kitchen.

'Jack Dougan?'

Gareth got an ice lolly out of the freezer.

'Yes.'

'But he's supposed to have gone. For good.'

Gareth shrugged his shoulders. 'Well, he's here now.'

'Where? In the living room?'

Gareth nodded casually. He'd barely got used to having a real dad, so what was the big deal about getting a last-minute substitute?

'I don't believe this,' groaned Kev. 'She said . . .'

'Mum's packed in smoking,' Gareth interrupted. In his eyes, that was obviously bigger news than the arrival of Jack Dougan. 'Look.'

He opened the lid of the swing-bin and pointed happily to the two full packs of cigarettes among the rubbish.

'You know what this means,' said Kev. 'I don't believe it!'

Plucking up the courage to face the stark truth, Kev opened the living-room door and walked in.

'Hi, Kev,' said Mum brightly. 'What was that I heard you saying about your report card?'

Kev chanced a sideways glance at Dougan. He was sitting beside Mum on the couch. His hand was brushing hers. Very lovey dovey, thought Kev.

'It's nothing,' said Kev broodily, slipping the report card behind his back.

This was between him and Mum, and had nothing to do with Plod.

'No, go on,' Mum urged. 'Tell me.' She turned to Dougan. 'He's started making a real effort at school.'

'It's all right,' said Kev. 'I'll tell you later.'

'Oh, don't mind Jack,' Mum told him. 'I've told him all about it.'

Kev flashed a hostile look at Dougan. What right did he have knowing their business?

'Go on,' said Mum. 'I'm all ears.'

'Mr Graham's recommending I go into the top set,' said Kev. 'For a trial period. They're going to review my progress at Christmas. If my work has continued to improve I can stay.'

'Oh Kev,' cried Mum, jumping up to hug him. 'That's marvellous news!'

Kev stood self-consciously rigid as Mum squeezed him. Did she have to? In front of Dougan too!

'What's he doing here?' Kev whispered.

Mum released him.

'I've got some news for you,' she said nervously. 'Jack's quit the Force.'

She stepped back, wondering how Kev was going to take it.

'Come again?'

It was Dougan's turn to explain.

'I gave the transfer a try,' he said. 'But my heart wasn't in it. Listen, Kev, I know this is hard for you, but I'm serious about your mum. When it came right down to it, Carol was more important than the job.'

'So you're not a copper any more?'

'Not for much longer. I've handed in my letter of resignation. A mate of mine runs a security firm. There's a job waiting for me.'

Kev's head was spinning.

'Hang on,' he said. 'This doesn't mean . . . You're not going to . . .'

'Spit it out, Kev,' said Mum.

'You're not planning to move in together?'

Dougan looked at Mum and smiled.

'It's on the cards,' he answered. 'There's plenty of room for the four of us at my place.'

Kev grabbed the back of an armchair. It was as if he was being dragged into a deep, dark whirlpool of lies and betrayals. This was supposed to be over. Now they were talking about leaving the Diamond.

'Never,' he murmured.

'Now now, Kev,' said Mum. 'Don't go over the top. There's still a lot of talking to be done. Just think about it. You're always saying the Diamond's a dump and Jack's got a lovely house in Old Roan. It could be a new start.'

'No way!' said Kev, his voice harsher and angrier.

'I know it's a big step,' said Dougan soothingly. 'So we won't be rushing into anything. You'll have plenty of time to get used to it.'

'That's just it,' cried Kev. 'I don't want to get used to it. I *won't* get used to it.'

He turned to make his escape.

'Kev,' Mum called after him. 'Don't do this. Stay and talk.'

'What, with him here? Forget it.'

'Carol,' Dougan said. 'Maybe I should go.'

'Forget it,' said Kev. 'I'm the one who's leaving.'

'Kevin!' cried Mum.

But Kev was already half-way down the hall. Pausing only to fling his report card on the floor, he ran off down the street.

So she wants a cosy little family, does she, Kev thought. Just her, Dougan, Gareth and me. Well forget it, Mum, I don't want any part of it. Got that, you can count me out.

Kev was at the top of Owen Avenue before he realized he had nowhere to go. Dad's flat was off limits since their row outside Mr Gulaid's shop and Mum would soon be on to Uncle Dave and Aunty Pat to see if he'd gone round there. As his anger subsided he came to a simple conclusion: it was lousy being a kid. You had no place of your own to hide when the going got tough. Guessing that Mum might come looking for him, he decided to avoid his usual haunts. He eventually found himself wandering past the fire station.

'Kevin?' came a voice. 'Is that you?'

'Oh, hi there, Ronnie.'

The team manager had poked his head out between the giant shuttered doors.

'What are you doing all the way down here?'

'Just walking.'

'Is that all there is to it? You look upset.'

Kev shrugged.

'Why don't you come and have a look round?' Ronnie suggested. 'It's quiet just now, so you'll be all right. Have you ever been round a fire station?'

Kev shook his head.

'Come on then.'

Ronnie gave him the grand tour. Where the fire-fighters ate, where they slept, the appliance and breathing apparatus. He even let him have a couple of goes down the pole.

'So what's eating you?' Ronnie asked finally. 'You were happy as Larry on Sunday. Is it your dad again?'

Kev shook his head.

'Not this time. It's Mum.'

There, he'd said it.

'Why, what's up?'

Kev hesitated.

'It's OK if you don't want to talk,' said Ronnie.

'No, I don't mind,' said Kev. 'She's got this feller . . .'

'Jack Dougan? Yes, I know him.'

'How?'

'We deal with the police all the time in this job.'

'Oh,' said Kev. 'What do you think of him?'

'Seems all right. A bit strait-laced.'

'How do you mean?'

Ronnie smiled. 'Goes by the book. He's pretty quiet really.'

Kev was hoping for something he could use, like he was corrupt or something. The sort of thing you saw in films.

'Is he married?'

This was Kev's last hope. He had a secret family somewhere. He'd seen that in a film as well.

'Divorced.'

'Oh.'

'You don't like him much, do you, Kev?'

Kev shook his head.

'I hate him.'

'Why?'

'I don't know. It's wrong. Mum's already married.'

Ronnie smiled. 'Not for long, though.'

'No,' Kev admitted. 'Not for long.'

'What is it you don't like about him?'

Kev frowned.

'I just don't.'

'Is it because he isn't your dad?'

Kev stared at Ronnie. How did he know all this stuff?

'I had a step-dad,' said Ronnie.

'You?'

Kev imagined older people didn't have problems.

'Yes, me. My real dad died in an accident on the docks when I was little. Mum was alone for a few years, then she remarried. It was years before I even spoke to her new husband.'

'But you did in the end?'

'Only when it was too late. He was dying of cancer by then. He was a lovely bloke, but I never gave him a chance. I regret it now.'

Kev shook his head. 'I hope you're not trying to get me to give Dougan a chance.'

'That's your business,' said Ronnie. 'I'm just telling you about myself.'

Kev grinned. 'Sure, Ronnie, I really believe you.'

'Suit yourself, Kev lad,' said Ronnie. 'No skin off my nose. So what are you going to do now?'

'I'd better get back,' Kev replied. 'Mum'll be getting worried.'

'Big game this Sunday,' said Ronnie, seeing Kev out of the station. 'Are you ready for it?'

Typical, thought Kev, one knock and Ronnie thinks I'm going to fold.

'Of course I am,' Kev told him firmly. 'Championship or bust.'

'That's the spirit,' said Ronnie. 'And good luck with your parent problems.'

He'd said it light-heartedly enough so Kev wouldn't be offended.

'Thanks,' said Kev. 'I'll need it.'

# Four

*Mum didn't say much when I got in last night. She just handed me my report card and told me how pleased she was and that I needed to keep up the good work. Keep up the good work! That's rich coming from her. I just want her to be proud of me, to make a real fuss of me. I'm fed up of being the Kid from Hell. I want her to boast about me like she does about Gareth. So there I am ready for my big moment and Plod turns up to steal my thunder. What a kick in the teeth that was! Then comes the master stroke – we're going to move in with him. She even thinks I'll be prepared to go because I grumble about the Diamond. Honestly, sometimes I think she doesn't know me at all. The Diamond is a dump, but it isn't the houses I'll miss, or the scabby shops, or the litter and graffiti. I've got mates now, mates like I never had in my life before. For the first time in my life I'm actually starting to feel like I belong. Now Plod has plans to ruin it all. Well, I've got news for you, Dougan, you'll have to drag me screaming out of here.*

# Five

Thursday evening was Bashir's birthday and the event was graced with the first fine weather in weeks. The party spilled out into the Gulaids' front garden. Ratso, of course, provided the music.

'Put *Three Lions* on again,' said Jamie.

Ratso obliged and soon the whole party were dancing up and down belting out the chorus. Mr and Mrs Gulaid, Kev's mum, Ronnie, Uncle Dave, Aunty Pat and Cheryl stood at the front door, watching the boys' antics.

'Are you nervous about Sunday?' asked Gord as the excitement died down.

'Me?' said Kev. 'A bit.'

'What?' came a voice. 'The Guv'nor, nervous?'

It was Dave Lafferty.

'Dave,' said Bashir. 'You made it.'

'Of course,' said Dave. I'm not going to forget my old mates, am I?'

Dave had got in at the Bluecoat school. What with that and the School of Excellence, he didn't seem to be around much.

'So what about the championship?' he asked.

'I just wish it was a straight fight between us and the Liver Bird,' said Jamie. 'Imagine if we won our game, but Longmoor took the title anyway. Or even Ajax. We'd be gutted.'

Bashir and Liam nodded in agreement.

'There's no point thinking like that,' said Kev. 'We've got to do our own job. It's all we can do. If the other result goes against us, it's just hard luck.'

'And you'll be saying that at final whistle on Sunday?' asked Daz. 'I doubt it.'

Kev smiled. 'I doubt it too. I'd be devastated, but the Longmoor result is out of our hands. We've just got to make sure we win our own game.'

'You've got it in you,' said Dave. 'Those twins you've got playing up front are good.'

'Liam and Conor,' said Kev. 'Yes, they're really coming on.'

'Another reason to get the coaching staff to take a look at my old team,' said Dave.

Kev's heart kicked. If only!

'Wouldn't it be great if we could bury Costello and Co?' said Chris. 'You know, ten-nil or something.'

'Hello,' said Jamie. 'Speak of the devil.'

Costello and Brain Damage were walking past. Carl Bain, Mattie Hughes and Tez Cronin were with them.

'Enjoy yourselves now, Diamonds,' said Costello. 'You won't be smiling on Sunday.'

His words drew catcalls and whistles from the Diamonds.

'Get lost, Costello,' said Kev. 'We'll sort you out down Jacob's Lane.'

'What,' Brain Damage countered. 'Like you sorted us in the Cup?'

Kev hated being reminded of their exit at the hands of the Liver Bird and took a couple of steps towards the front gate.

'Leave it,' said Jamie. 'We'll do our talking on the football field.'

Kev nodded. He was about to return to the party when a familiar car pulled up. It was Ramage's white BMW. Dad was at the wheel.

'Having a nice time?' asked Ramage.

Mr Gulaid hurried to the gate.

'This is my son's birthday party,' he said angrily. 'Now go away.'

'It's a free country,' said Ramage coolly. 'We've got every right to park where we want.'

While Ramage and Mr Gulaid faced up to one another, Kev and Dad exchanged glances. There was an ocean of mistrust between them.

'Whatever argument you have with me,' Mr Gulaid said, 'my son isn't part of it. Now please go or I will phone the police.'

'Fond of that, aren't you?' sneered Ramage.

'I have told you before,' Mr Gulaid retorted, 'whoever phoned the police, it wasn't me.'

Ramage shook his head dismissively, then tapped Dad on the shoulder.

'Drive on, Tony,' he said. 'I want to call in on my mother.'

'I see some things don't change,' said Dave Lafferty.

The BMW moved the few doors up Owen Avenue to Brain Damage's house. Seeing Dad still sitting in the car, Kev decided it was time to have it out with him.

'Kev,' said Mum, seeing him opening the gate. 'Where are you going?'

'There's something I've got to do,' he told her. 'I won't be a minute.'

He approached the car and tapped on the driver's window. Dad lowered it.

'What is it, Kev?'

'That was a rotten trick, trying to ruin Bashir's birthday party.'

'It's business,' said Dad.

'Well, it's pretty rotten business,' said Kev. 'No wonder Mum wants out.'

'What do you mean?'

Kev was going to enjoy turning the knife, even if it hurt himself to do it.

'Only that Dougan's asked her to move in with him.'

'Dougan, but I thought . . .'

'That you'd driven him away?' asked Kev. 'Looks like you failed, Dad, just like you'll fail with Mr Gulaid.'

Dad's eyes narrowed.

'I wouldn't be too sure about that, Kev.'

It was Kev's turn to be surprised.

'What's that supposed to mean?'

Dad's expression changed. He realized he'd said too much.

'What are you going to do?'

As he pressed Dad for information, Kev noticed a strange smell.

'Here's Lee,' said Dad. 'I think you'd better get back to your party.'

'Please, Dad,' Kev begged. 'Don't do Ramage's dirty work. Please.'

There it was again. That smell. Petrol. He stared at Dad.

'Come on, Tony,' said Ramage, getting in the car. 'We've got a lot to do.'

The smell wasn't coming from the car's fuel tank. It was too strong for that.

'Dad,' Kev cried, old nightmares returning. 'I know what you're going to do.'

'Kev,' Dad snapped, seeing Lee Ramage staring questioningly at him. 'I've got to go.'

As the car pulled away, Kev stood in the street staring after it. He had never been so afraid in his life.

# Six

'What was all that about?' asked Mum.

'I told Dad about Jack Dougan,' Kev replied.

He was trying to work out how to put his plan into action.

'How did he react?' asked Mum.

'How do you think? He was upset.'

'You mean he started bawling and shouting,' said Mum.

'Not really, but he wasn't happy.'

'No,' said Mum. 'I understand that. It'll be wounded pride. He doesn't care for me any more, that's for sure.'

Kev stared at his feet.

'Mum,' he said, forcing out the words he hardly dared say. 'Dad's asked if I'd like to stop over at his place tonight. You said I could, remember.'

Somebody once said that if you're going to tell a lie, make it a big one. They didn't come much bigger than this.

'What, on a school day! I thought he'd forgotten all about it.'

'No, he says it's to make up for letting us down last time.'

'I don't know,' Mum said dubiously. 'And Gareth certainly isn't staying.'

'I don't think Gareth's bothered. Dad's getting him a present instead. Besides . . .' Kev's mind was working overtime. 'He's getting a film in. Its too old for Gareth.'

'How old's that?'

'A fifteen,' said Kev.

'Mm.'

Mum still wasn't convinced.

'Look, Mum,' said Kev. 'I know he's done lots of lousy things, but he's still my dad. And if we do move up to the Old Roan . . .'

That was the clincher. Even hinting that he might accept the move was bound to sway Mum.

'What about school?' Mum asked.

'I'll take my uniform with me,' said Kev, a little too hurriedly. 'I can go straight to school from Dad's flat.'

'I still don't know what's come over him,' said Mum. 'Discovering his parental responsibilities all of a sudden.'

'Like I said,' Kev told her. 'I think he's feeling a bit guilty.'

'Doesn't sound like Tony to me,' said Mum.

'It's OK though?'

Mum nodded. 'I suppose so. Just make sure you get to school on time.'

'I will, Mum. I won't let you down.'

He almost choked on the words.

'Right,' said Mum. 'The moment we get in, I'll pack your uniform. And you can tell your dad he's not making a habit of this.'

'Don't worry,' said Kev. 'I'm sure it'll be a one-off.'

Kev wiped his palms on his jeans. That's got over the first obstacle, he thought. Now for Mr Gulaid. He drew Bashir aside.

'Your dad isn't planning to stay at the shop again, is he?'

'I don't know. Probably. Why?'

'I think Dad and Ramage are planning something.'

'So does my father,' said Bashir. 'That's why he sleeps there.'

Kev thought about mentioning the petrol, but that

would really mean dropping Dad in it. No, better keep that bit of information under wraps.

'Is there no way you can persuade him to stay here tonight?' asked Kev.

Bashir's brow furrowed.

'Do you know something?' he asked.

'No,' said Kev. He was piling lie upon lie. 'But I know what he's capable of.'

'My dad is stubborn,' said Bashir.

'But if you really make a fuss,' said Kev. 'You know, it being your birthday and all.'

'I'll try,' said Bashir. 'But I've been trying for days. He won't listen. He just can't stand the idea of somebody trying to scare him off.'

The rest of the party passed in a haze. Kev didn't feel part of it any more. A couple of times he actually decided to tell Mum everything, but the idea of Dad being arrested again was just too much to bear. He felt a coward but he kept his secret. The plan was desperate, a bit crazy even. He was no detective. Where did he start? Did he hang round Dad's flat or Ramage's place? Or did he just keep watch on Mr Gulaid's shop? And was he going to stay up all night? But he had to go through with it. *Could* he stay up without falling asleep? He was scared. He felt completely out of his depth. But he had to stop Dad, and mad as the plan seemed, Kev couldn't see any other way.

# Seven

By half past seven that evening, Kev had even roped Jamie into his plan. Knowing he had to be mobile to stand any chance of tracking Dad down, he had sneaked his bike down to Jamie's. Jamie didn't even ask what it was all about. He was a true mate.

'There,' said Mum. 'That's your uniform, a toothbrush, your bus fare to school and a couple of pounds just in case. Oh, I forgot this.'

She handed him his report card. As Kev took it, he felt a twinge of conscience. There was Mum talking about new starts, and he was up to his neck in the old trouble.

'Still time to get a few more good comments,' she said.

Kev grimaced. Her face looked so trusting. He was feeling bad about lying to her.

'I think I might give your dad a ring,' she said. 'Just to make sure he understands how important it is to make sure you get to school on time.'

Kev nearly choked. 'Don't do that.'

'Why not?'

'Oh, come on, Mum, you'll only end up rowing with him.'

Mum hesitated.

'I suppose you're right.'

Kev breathed a sigh of relief. He knew the right buttons to press.

'I'll be off then.'

'OK, see you tomorrow teatime. Be good.'

She gave him a peck on the cheek. In return, Kev gave her a lopsided smile.

'See you, Mum.'

Giving her a last wave goodbye, Kev set off for Jamie's.

'Keep this for me,' he said when Jamie came to the door.

'What is it?'

'My uniform.'

'What do I do with it?'

Kev looked around. His eyes lighted on the old rabbit hutch.

'You don't use that, do you?'

'No, Snowball died.'

'That's it, then. Get me a bin bag and some Sellotape.'

'You what?'

'Just do it, will you?'

Jamie returned with the two items and Kev wrapped his holdall up in the bin bag before securing the neck with Sellotape.

'Stick it in the hutch for me,' said Kev. 'The bin bag should keep the rain out.'

He looked up at the grey clouds.

'Now, where's my bike?'

'There.'

It was propped against the wall round the corner.

'I wish I knew what you were up to,' said Jamie.

'No, you don't,' said Kev, straddling the bike.

'I bet it's exciting.'

Not the word I'd use, thought Kev, Terrifying's more like it.

'Well, good luck,' said Jamie. 'Whatever you're doing.'

Kev pedalled away, taking care to steer clear of Owen Avenue. He didn't want Mum spotting him. First stop was Dad's flat. The lights were out and there was no BMW parked in front. On to Ramage's place. It was the same story there. He was beginning to lose heart already.

You can't give up now, he told himself. This is important.

'The shop it is then,' said Kev, turning round and heading for South Parade.

All the shops were closed and shuttered. The Parade was deserted. But what about Mr Gulaid? Had Bashir persuaded him to stay away? There was only one way to find out. Pushing his bike out of sight, Kev picked up a couple of fragments of brick and crept towards the shop. Taking aim, he flung a piece of brick at the metal shutters and retired. Less than a minute later, the security door opened and Mr Gulaid appeared. He looked around for a few minutes, then returned inside. Kev heard the scrape of a lock. Mr Gulaid was shutting himself in.

'Why couldn't you listen?' sighed Kev. 'Why couldn't you just stay away?'

He was beginning to have even more doubts about his plan. As the hours ticked by and darkness fell, he was on the verge of going home and telling Mum more than once. About a quarter to ten he heard a car engine. He rode to the end of the Parade and looked down South Road. A white car was roaring past the Community Centre. His indecision fell away.

'It's them,' Kev said out loud.

Seeing the car turning towards Ramage's flat, he set off in pursuit. Suddenly, he didn't have a plan any more. He just wanted to stay close and keep tabs on them. He had to know what they were up to. As he turned left at the top of the road he saw the car parked outside the Liver Bird.

'I might have guessed you'd be here,' he said. It was the roughest pub on the estate and the landlord was a big mate of Ramage's. He'd helped pay for Costello and Co's footy strip. Still, if Dad and Ramage were in the pub, they couldn't be doing anybody any harm. Kev was about to find somewhere to continue his watch when he noticed the car's badge, a series of linked rings.

'Hang on,' he murmured. 'That isn't a BMW. It's an Audi.' He felt a hot rush through his body. 'You idiot, McGovern, you've got the wrong car.'

His heart kicked. I've blown it, he thought desperately. He had to get back to the Parade, and quick. Cycling furiously, he ate up the distance back to the shop, wishing away every single yard. As he passed McGaw's he cried out. It had happened. Dad was jumping into the car. The shop was already on fire.

'No!'

The car started to accelerate away from the shop. As it passed Kev, he was caught in its headlights. It screeched to a halt.

'Kev,' said Dad, completely taken aback by his son's presence. 'What on earth . . . ?'

'It's Mr Gulaid,' yelled Kev, the horror reducing his voice to a strangled shriek. 'He's in there.'

Dad stared at the blazing shop.

'He can't be.'

'He is, I tell you,' cried Kev, struggling to stay calm. 'He's been sleeping in the shop and all because of you.'

Ramage glared at Dad.

'Drive for goodness' sake, Tony. Can't you see the kid's making it up? He's always been like this. You've said so yourself.'

Dad hesitated.

'Please,' Kev begged. 'He could die in there.'

Dad's face had drained of colour.

'I can't take the risk, Lee. I've got to check.'

'Don't be an idiot,' said Ramage. 'If he is there, so what? It's his own stupid fault.'

Dad jumped out of the car.

'What are you going to do?' asked Ramage, 'In a few

minutes the place could be crawling with police cars and fire engines.'

'We've still got that lump hammer in the back from when I changed the wheel. I've got to get those shutters open.'

'You're mad,' said Ramage.

'Maybe,' said Dad, searching for the hammer. 'But I can't kill a man. Lee, give me your mobile.'

'What for?'

'What do you think? I'm phoning the fire brigade.'

'Not on this phone,' said Ramage. 'It could be traced.'

'Kev,' said Dad, handing him some change. 'Run to the phone box at the top of the Parade. Call nine-nine-nine.'

When Kev returned Ramage was in the driver's seat, revving the BMW impatiently.

'This is your last chance to get in the car,' said Ramage. 'I'm not hanging round here to get caught.'

'Then go,' Dad told him, taking the hammer from the boot. 'I'm staying.'

Kev heard Ramage take off but he didn't take any notice. He was too busy staring at the flames licking under the security shutters.

'Hurry, Dad.'

Dad raced to the shutters and started beating away at the catch.

'He's rigged something up,' he cried. 'It's padlocked from the inside. I don't know if I'm doing any good.'

'Just keep going,' pleaded Kev. 'You set fire to it, didn't you? There has to be a way.'

'Pouring petrol in is a lot easier than breaking in,' Dad panted. 'We failed the last time we tried.'

'Keep trying,' Kev pleaded.

In the distance he could hear the wail of sirens. Dad

looked up, then continued hitting the catch. Suddenly it gave.

'Got it!'

Wrapping his jacket round his hands to protect them, Dad gripped the red-hot shutters and forced them up. A moment later he had vanished into the smoke and flames.

The police and fire brigade arrived at about the same time. Kev was relieved to see the familiar figure of Ronnie Mintoe jump from the fire engine.

'Kev, what are you doing here?'

'I'll tell you later,' Kev sobbed. 'Mr Gulaid's in there. My dad went in after him. You've got to save them.'

'Tell me the truth, Kev, there really are two men in there?'

Kev nodded.

'Please, you've got to help them.'

Within moments water was being trained on the flames and a team of firefighters was making its way into the fire wearing breathing apparatus. Ronnie stood next to Kev with his arms round him.

'They will find them, won't they?'

'These lads are the best, Kev,' said Ronnie. 'They'll get them out.'

The search seemed to take ages, but could only have taken seconds.

'Here they come,' shouted a policeman.

Sure enough, dark figures were emerging from the flames. The firefighters were leading two men from the inferno. One was walking, carrying the other in his arms. Kev tried to run forward.

'No,' said Ronnie, restraining him. 'Let the paramedics do their work.'

By now Kev could make out the faces of the two men. Dad was lowering Mr Gulaid on to a stretcher. Dad was coughing and spluttering, but he looked OK. That was more than could be said for Mr Gulaid.

## Eight

Kev was sitting huddled on a red plastic chair in the bare hospital waiting room when Mum arrived. Mrs Gulaid and Bashir had beaten her by about five minutes and were talking to a doctor.

'What's happened?' Mum asked. 'I got a phone call, but it didn't make any sense. Why aren't you at Tony's?'

Kev couldn't look at her.

'I wasn't at Dad's. I lied to you.'

'Then where were you? What's this got to do with Mr Gulaid?' A flash of realization crossed her face. 'Oh no!'

Kev could see Mrs Gulaid and Bashir coming down the corridor. He wished he could sink through the floor.

'It's Tony, isn't it?' Mum asked. 'He did it. He torched the shop.'

Kev nodded miserably.

'But why didn't you tell me? How could you think of trying to sort it out yourself?'

Kev chewed nervously at the collar of his jacket.

'I didn't want Dad to get put away. I thought . . .'

That's when he broke down, tears spilling down his cheeks. He hated himself for crying, but this time there was no time to prevent it. Mum stopped asking questions. Instead, she folded him in her arms. He sat curled up that way for a long time, then Mum slowly eased herself away from him and stood up. She was talking to Mrs Gulaid.

'How is he?' Mum asked.

'He has one burn on his arm,' said Mrs Gulaid. 'Nothing serious. They've got an oxygen mask on him and they're testing his . . .' She looked at Bashir for help.

'They're monitoring his oxygen saturation levels,' said Bashir.

His English was better than his mother's.

'But he's going to be all right?'

'Yes,' said Mrs Gulaid. 'He'll be fine. They're keeping him in overnight.' She looked at Mum. 'I suppose you know who did this?'

Mum lowered her eyes. 'I've worked it out. Oh, Zaynab, I'm so sorry.'

'It's not your fault,' said Mrs Gulaid. 'Or Kevin's. Your son probably saved my husband's life.'

Kev saw Bashir looking at him. He didn't feel like a hero at all.

'And Tony?' said Mum.

'The police have got him,' said Kev, speaking for the first time since the Gulaids came over. 'He can't get out of it this time.'

'This is really serious,' said Mum, 'but I can hardly believe it, not even of Tony. He's a hard man, but this . . . It's evil.'

'Dad didn't know anybody was inside,' said Kev. 'He's the one who got Mr Gulaid out.'

'Is that true?' Mum asked.

'Yes,' said Mrs Gulaid. 'Mohammed told me.'

'He's able to talk then?'

'A little, but it makes him cough terribly.'

—— 121 ——

Mum dabbed at her eyes with a handkerchief. 'This is so dreadful. I can't tell you how sorry I am.'

Mrs Gulaid smiled. 'I told you. It isn't your fault.'

'But you must hate the estate. You've had so much trouble.'

'I would like to leave, yes, that is true. Bashir and I are going to my sister's tonight. I don't feel safe in the house.'

'But you will be back?'

Mrs Gulaid shook her head. 'I don't think so. I've had enough.'

Kev's heart turned over. He looked at Bashir who returned his look.

'I can't blame you for being angry and scared,' said Mum. 'But don't give up on us. We're not all like my ex-husband.'

Mrs Gulaid nodded. 'I know.'

While their mothers talked Kev and Bashir slipped away to the far end of the corridor.

'I didn't want this to happen,' said Kev. 'I tried to warn you at the party.'

'Your father is a bad man,' said Bashir.

Kev nodded sadly.

'I know.'

'No,' said Bashir. 'You don't. He is refusing to give the police the name of the other man.'

'You mean he's covering for Ramage?'

It was Bashir's turn to nod.

'But that's crazy,' said Kev. 'I mean, he actually saved your dad. Ramage would have left him to die.'

Bashir listened coldly to Kev's words. 'He still won't give the police his name.'

'But Ramage will get off scot-free.'

Bashir dug his hands in his pockets. 'He always does.'

Kev cleared his throat then asked: 'You're angry with me, aren't you?'

'I think you were foolish,' Bashir replied. 'You should have told the police. Imagine what would have happened if your father had left with Ramage. My dad could be dead.'

Kev shuddered. Bashir was right. He'd risked Mr Gulaid's life, and all because of his stupid loyalty to Dad.

'Is it true, Bash, are you going for good?'

Bashir shrugged.

Kev was desperate for a sign of their old friendship.

'Can you forgive me?'

Mrs Gulaid was coming down the corridor towards them.

'Bashir,' she said. 'It is time to go.'

'Bash,' Kev repeated. 'Can you forgive me?'

Bashir stared at him for a few moments.

'I don't know, Guv, I just don't know.'

# Nine

*I went past Bashir's house again this afternoon, but there was nobody in. I can't forget the way he looked at me. Like I was a complete traitor, the lowest form of life. He's right of course. I've let everybody down. What was I doing trying to handle something like that by myself? Who do I think I am, Superman? Now I've lost Bashir's friendship forever. And on the same day I lost Dad too. He's going to go down for years. He's determined to carry the can all by himself. Even after Ramage cleared off and abandoned him, he still refuses to grass. I feel like I could roll over and die. I mean, I did*

—— 123 ——

*everything I could to help, but it's all gone wrong. What is it about me? Why does everything I touch go wrong? And how come the bad guys always win? Ramage is never going to get his come-uppance. He's going to run the Diamond forever. It's sick. I found out who'd been phoning the police as well. It was Mr McGaw. Seems he feels guilty about Mr Gulaid, so he's been telling everybody. He says he isn't afraid of Ramage. I just wonder if he isn't too brave for his own good.*

*Still, if there's one thing I've learned out of all this, it's who really matters to me. It's always been Dad this and Dad that, but who was there at the hospital, and who is it that listens without screaming her head off? Mum, that's who. She's not just better than Dad, she's stronger too. She wouldn't let somebody like Ramage run her life. She deserves a bit of happiness, and if that means I've got to put up with Plod, well, maybe that's what I've got to do.*

*Ronnie's just been on the phone, asking me how I am. I started off by telling him I didn't want to play tomorrow, but he's argued me round. He's right, of course. Staying away from the match won't do any good. I'll still pull out all the stops to win it, but it won't be the same without Bash. Oh, what the heck! You can't have everything. I should know that by now. I'm a survivor. I've never gone under before, and I don't intend to start now.*

# Ten

Next morning, Kev was up with the larks. *Before* them actually. As the dawn came up, grey and drizzly over the Diamond, he was channel-surfing listlessly. He chanced on a weather forecast and listened grimly as the presenter pointed out a huge bank of rain over Ireland. It was expected over Liverpool about kick-off time.

'Well, thanks a lot,' he grumbled.

Hearing footsteps on the stairs, he looked round. It was Mum.

'Kev,' she said. 'Do you know the time?'

He nodded. 'I couldn't sleep so I got up.'

Mum smiled. 'You, unable to sleep? This is a first. Excited about the match are you?'

Kev frowned. 'Not really. I was thinking about Bashir.'

Mum realized she'd said the wrong thing.

'Oh.'

'I really messed up this time, didn't I?'

'You meant well,' said Mum, sitting on the arm of his chair in her dressing gown. 'Your dad's the one who's really to blame. And that Lee Ramage. It makes my blood boil that he's going to get away with it. Trust Tony to cover for him.'

'What's going to happen to Dad?'

Mum took Kev's hand.

'There's no easy way to say this. He's going to prison.'

'Yes, I'd worked that out. Will I be able to see him?'

'Of course you will,' said Mum. 'He'll be out on bail until the trial.'

'He might not want to see me though,' said Kev. 'I'm the one who's put him inside.'

'No,' said Mum. 'He's managed that all by himself, and if he's any sort of man he'll never cut himself off from his children.'

Not wanting to show his feelings, Kev looked away and clicked round again until he came across a local news bulletin. The events at Mr Gulaid's shop were the third item.

'Something else we're going to have to tough out,' said Mum.

Kev nodded.

'We've had plenty of practice, haven't we?'

Mum tousled his hair.

'You can say that again. Do you want some breakfast?'

In the films people usually shake their heads and say they don't want anything. But Kev was ravenous. He wanted to be guilt-ridden and unable to eat. That's how people acted on the telly. But it just wasn't him. No matter how bad things got, the fire still burned bright inside him. He was a survivor all right, and you don't survive on an empty stomach.

'Wouldn't mind a bite to eat.'

'Egg, bacon . . .'

Kev nodded.

'Fried bread . . .'

Another nod.

'Toast . . .'

'Any beans?'

Mum laughed. 'When I saw you sitting there, I wondered if you were feeling off colour. I shouldn't have worried.'

Kev grinned, but as Mum walked into the kitchen to start the breakfast the smile vanished. He had an appetite for food, but what about football?

Four hours later, the Diamonds were battling through pouring rain. Conditions at kick-off had been so bad, the league committee had seriously considered abandoning play.

Only a plea from both managers had persuaded them to go ahead, but they were probably regretting it within minutes of the start. What should have been a game of skill between two of the league's top sides was rapidly turning into a war. There were grudges to be settled in every area of the pitch. Kev had been pitted against Costello and Brain Damage for the best part of two years. John O'Hara and Carl Bain also had a score to settle. Not only was Carl an ex-Diamond and a turncoat. His mum and John's dad had gone out for a brief period, something both boys resented. Another ex-Diamond Mattie Hughes had it in for Gord. And so it went on. Twenty-two boys who lived just doors from each other but may as well have been from different planets. Brain Damage set the tone after five minutes by up-ending Jamie just outside the penalty area.

'Dirty fouling get!' snapped Kev.

Brain Damage simply grinned, something that was calculated to set Kev's blood boiling.

'You wait till you have the ball,' Kev warned him. 'You want rough stuff? We'll give you rough stuff.'

'Do your worst, McGovern,' said Brain Damage.

Which is exactly what Kev had planned, until Liam shot him a warning glance.

'Cool it, Guv,' he whispered. 'The ref's watching you.'

Kev glanced in the ref's direction. The thought of blowing the Diamonds' title hopes by getting sent off sobered him up. He gave Liam a little nod to show he'd got his temper back under control.

'I wish Bashir was here,' said Liam. 'We're getting no service at all down the left-hand side.'

Kev let the comment pass in silence. He felt guilty enough about Bashir's absence without Liam having to remind him about it.

'Come on, Joey,' Kev shouted. 'Run the ball.'

Ronnie was trying Joey out as a winger but it wasn't working at all. Joey had neither the pace nor the accuracy of crossing to make any impact on a tough, well-organized Liver Bird defence.

'Oh Joey,' groaned Liam as he ran the ball out of play.

'Sorry,' said Joey.

The Liver Bird were having more success up the other end, where a series of long balls out of defence were causing all sorts of problems, the main reason being a fast, slippery striker by the name of Wayne Bowe. He was sharp and inventive and seemed capable of turning the most speculative boot out of defence into a goal-threatening move. After his third shot on goal in as many minutes, Daz stormed out to give his defence a rollicking.

'So who was supposed to pick him up this time?' he demanded. 'Gord, I thought you were marking him.'

'I'm trying,' he replied. 'It's easier said than done.'

Alerted to the tough time Gord was having, Kev told Chris to take Wayne Bowe.

'Stick to him like a leech,' Kev ordered. 'Just stop him. I don't care how.'

That too was easier said than done. After a quiet spell Bowe set off on a mesmerizing run, turning Chris inside out before delivering a raking cross into the goalmouth. Daz was just collecting the ball when Brain Damage came storming in and flattened the big Diamonds' keeper. The ref gave a free kick but as he took it, Daz was still aggrieved.

'He should have been booked for that,' he complained.

Kev and Ratso started some promising moves in the Liver Bird half, culminating in a diving header by Conor that missed the right-hand post by inches. But still the pattern of the game was being broken up by a rash of niggly fouls. Midway through the half the ref showed his first yellow card. The culprit was Tez Cronin who had dead-legged Ratso.

'About time,' said Kev as the ref took Cronin's name.

Even then the rough stuff didn't stop. Going for a corner, Daz was brought crashing to the ground a second time. On this occasion it was Costello who'd barged him.

'How's about some protection, ref?' Daz grumbled.

But the ref signalled to him to stop moaning and get on with the game.

'Well, if he isn't going to put a stop to it,' Kev seethed, 'then we will. Come on, lads,' he shouted. 'Get stuck in. An eye for an eye, a tooth for a tooth. Fight for every inch of ground.'

It was a typical call to arms, but it didn't have quite the result Kev was expecting. If anything the foul count rose and this time the Diamonds were being penalized as often as the Liver Bird. With ten minutes to go until half-time a frustrated Chris Power brought Wayne Bowe down just outside the penalty area. It was in a central position, a dangerous place to concede a free kick.

'What do you think you're doing, Chris?' asked Kev.

'What you told us to do,' Chris answered shortly. 'I got stuck in.'

Ouch, thought Kev, I asked for that. It had seemed like a good game plan at the time, but the Diamonds were getting bogged down in a war of attrition. Their usual game of pass and move was suffering.

'Watch this, McGovern,' said Costello as he placed the ball. 'Wayne's got a shot like a demon.'

Bowe took a short run up and struck the ball with his

—— 129 ——

instep, sending it looping over the Diamonds' wall. For a moment it looked like the ball was going over, but it dipped sharply and bounced in off the bar. The Liver Bird went wild.

'See that,' Brain Damage taunted Kev. 'Your old man's a loser, now you're a loser just like him. How does it feel, *loser?*'

For once, Kev had no answer. Just as the Diamonds' fortunes hit their low point, Ratso treated them to some good news.

'Hey lads,' he shouted. 'Here's the cavalry.'

The cavalry came in the slight form of Bashir.

'You came,' Kev exclaimed. 'Does that mean . . . ?'

'You were a bit stupid,' said Bashir. 'But without you my dad would probably be dead. I'm here to play.'

'We certainly need something,' said Kev.

'I agree,' said Bashir. 'One thing, Guv. You do know you're playing right into their hands?'

'How do you mean?'

'I'll tell you what he means,' said Ronnie, advancing down the touch-line. 'It's like D-Day out there. Up to your necks in muck and bullets. What do you think you're doing, Kev?'

Kev looked at Brain Damage and Costello, still gloating over their goal. Ronnie was right. They loved nothing better than a good fight. And that's all the Diamonds had given them so far. No skill, no tactics, just a fight.

'I've been an idiot, haven't I?' Kev groaned. 'Even though I said I wouldn't, I let them get to me.'

'Fine,' said Ronnie, only half-seriously. 'Now we're all agreed that you're an idiot, go and do something about it.'

In what remained of the half, Kev tried to get the

Diamonds playing, but the Liver Bird's gamesmanship was making it difficult. When Costello pulled Conor's shirt to stop a promising run, Conor reacted with a push. Both players were booked. On the stroke of half-time Jamie almost equalized when he smashed Kev's slide-rule pass against the bar. But almost wasn't good enough, as Costello pointed out.

He walked right up to Kev, forming the scoreline with his fingers.

'One-nil, McGovern, one-nil. How does it feel to be a loser?'

Kev bit his tongue, but it felt bad. Really bad.


# *Eleven*

'You want my honest opinion?' said Ronnie. 'We've got our backs against the wall. In case you've forgotten, this is what we need to win the championship, this is the dream scenario. We win. Longmoor fail to win. That puts us level on points, but with a superior goal difference. Result? We take the championship.'

The Diamonds waited for the punch-line. When it came it was blunt and to the point.

'But,' Ronnie continued, stabbing the air with his finger, 'the way it stands, we're losing one-nil and Longmoor are leading by the same margin. Result?'

Kev finished the speech for him. 'We lose.'

'Exactly,' said Ronnie. 'Give that lad a pat on the back. Got it in one, Kev. We lose. Did that sink in, lads? We *lose* the championship'

He inspected the faces of his players. 'Look at me, lads. Do I look like somebody who enjoys losing?'

'No, Ronnie,' one or two of the lads muttered.

'So what the flipping heck was that?' roared Ronnie. 'The dirtiest team in the league start kicking lumps out of you, and how do you respond? You kick back. What are you, donkeys?'

He glared at Kev.

'Look, Kev,' he said, softening his voice, 'I know you're competitive, but you're going about it the wrong way. The only way to beat a fouling outfit like this is to play your own game. Out-pass them, out-manoeuvre them, out-*think* them.'

'Behave,' Conor retorted. 'If some meff starts on me, I'll give as good as I get.'

Murmurs of agreement ran through the team. Kev saw Bashir looking at him, willing him to support Ronnie.

'Hang on a minute,' said Kev. 'Ronnie's right.'

'I've said it before,' Conor announced, 'and I'll say it again, the Guv'nor's going soft.'

'Wrong,' said Kev. 'Soft in the head is what I've been. I hate the Liver Bird. They're the lowest form of life. So what did I do? I fought them. But there are different ways of fighting. You don't have to dive in with your fists flying every time.'

Conor gave him a sceptical frown. Chris and Ant followed suit.

'Let's just try it, eh?' said Kev. 'Give it fifteen minutes. We move the ball around, run at them, put in quality crosses. For the last month every game has been a blood and snot scrap. But it's the last day, so let's turn on the style.'

He waited for a response.

'Come on, lads, give it a go, eh?'

'OK,' said Conor. 'Fifteen minutes.'

'Right,' said Ronnie. 'One change. Bashir, you're on for Joey. We need a left-sided player who can go past them. Fancy it, son?'

Bashir nodded. It was just what he wanted, a chance to put one over on the Liver Bird. 'Let's destroy them,' he said.

As Kev followed Bashir on to the pitch he was given another incentive to beat the Liver Bird. Dave Lafferty had just arrived with a balding man in his late forties.

*Is that him?* Kev mouthed.

'Guv,' said Dave, smiling. 'Meet Tommy. He's on the coaching staff at Everton.'

'So,' said Tommy. 'You're the Guv'nor. I've heard a lot about you.'

Kev stared at Dave, then turned to Ratso.

'Rats,' Kev hissed. 'I know this is unusual, but is that tape of yours ready?'

'What, *The Final Countdown*?'

Kev nodded.

'Let's run on to a rousing fanfare.'

Ratso grinned.

'Got you.'

As news of the scout's presence ran through the team, they weren't just fired up, they were *on fire*. Jamie and Bashir were skipping past defenders at will and Jimmy was going on the overlap, whipping in dangerous crosses. The Liver Bird were hanging on by the skin of their teeth. But there were still no goals to show for all the pressure.

'How are they keeping the ball out?' panted an anguished Liam as yet another effort was blocked.

'Just keep pressing,' said Kev. 'They'll crack.'

And crack they did. Ten minutes into the half, Bashir nutmegged Brain Damage and beat Tez Cronin and

Luke Costello with a meandering dribble that took him to the bye-line.

'Get it over,' yelled Kev. 'Now!'

But Bashir had glimpsed Ratso haring into the box. Cutting the ball back he set Ratso up with a clear shot on goal. Not known for his finishing, Ratso shut his eyes and went for power.

'Goal!'

He opened his eyes to see the net bulging.

One-one.

Another run five minutes later forced Carl Bain into a desperate tackle in the area. Kev converted the resulting penalty.

Two-one.

'Keep it going,' said Kev. 'No mercy.'

And there wasn't. First Liam then Conor scored from corners. At four-one the Diamonds were feeling confident about their own game, but what about the Longmoor-Ajax contest?

'It's one-one,' shouted Ronnie. 'Ajax are back in it.'

'We're going to do it,' cried Kev. 'I can feel it. We've got a hand on the trophy.'

But the Diamonds' grip was about to slip, and all thanks to a show of temper from an unexpected source. The flare-up came when Costello floated in a corner kick. Sticking to the game plan of intimidating the Diamonds' keeper, Brain Damage barged Daz into the post. Incensed at yet another blatant foul, Daz crashed his fist into Brain Damage's face. Realizing what he'd done, Daz looked to see where the ref was. He was out of luck.

He'd landed his punch right in front of the official.

'Oh no, ref,' begged Daz. 'I was only defending myself.'

'You raised your hands, son,' said the ref, reaching for a card.

The colour was red.

'You're off.'

As Daz trudged miserably off the pitch, Ronnie examined his options. He'd already substituted his reserve keeper, Joey Bannen. The only other player with goalkeeping experience was Dougie Long.

'John,' he called to the midfielder. 'You're off. Dougie's coming on to play in goal.'

'Are you sure about this?' asked Dougie. 'When I played for Red House we conceded more goals than any other team.'

'That was a year ago,' said Ronnie. 'And you had a lousy side in front of you.'

Dougie jogged uncertainly towards his goal.

'Don't worry, Dougie,' said Kev. 'We'll try to protect you.'

But for all their good intentions, the Diamonds were in trouble. The midfield was suddenly lightweight and disjointed and the Liver Bird started attacking in numbers.

After a couple of minutes of sustained pressure, they broke through, Costello scoring with a diving header.

'Four-two,' said Kev. 'We've still got a two-goal cushion.'

But within minutes it was down to one. Jimmy slipped, allowing Wayne Bowe to burst through and beat Dougie with a powerful shot.

Four-three and the Diamonds were rocking.

'Don't get rattled,' Kev told his team. 'Just hold on. Ajax are still holding Longmoor.'

'Better than that,' shouted Ronnie. 'They're two-one up.'

'Hear that?' Kev yelled. 'If we can hang on the title's ours.'

Seconds later the news got even better. Ajax had gone three-one up. The news steadied the Diamonds' nerves. With Kev pulling all the strings in midfield, they were beginning to defend solidly and Jamie and Bashir were still giving them problems on the break.

'How long?' asked Ratso. 'I'm done in.'

'Two minutes,' said Kev. 'Just two minutes to hold out.'

But with a minute on the watch, disaster stuck. Wayne Bowe broke through on the left and was going for goal. He lobbed Dougie, but just as he was about to celebrate the equalizer Chris managed to get a hand to the ball and palm it over. It was a desperate effort and it was going to cost him. The ref sent off the second Diamonds' player of the match.

'Don't feel bad,' said Kev. 'You had no choice.'

Chris nodded, but he still felt gutted. A marksman like Bowe was sure to convert the penalty.

'Just do your best, Dougie,' Kev advised. 'Choose which way you're going and launch yourself.'

Dougie nodded, but as he walked back to his line he looked anything but confident. After all, he'd already conceded two goals since coming on. Then came the surprise move that had everybody talking.

'My kick, Wayne,' said Costello, nudging the striker out of the way.

'Since when did you take penalties?' demanded Bowe.

'Since you missed that one against Warbreck,' said Costello. 'I'm captain and I give the orders. I'm taking it. I want to see the Diamonds' faces when I win the championship for us.'

He took a short run up and stared theatrically at the

right-hand post. Dougie knew immediately he was going to put it to his left. Remembering what Kev had said, Dougie threw himself to his left and . . . pushed the ball round the post.

'What a save!' cried Ratso.

'Dougie,' said Kev. 'You're my hero.'

'Hang on,' said Dougie. 'There's still the corner to defend.'

But as the ball came over he was equal to it, punching out with confidence. As Kev set off after it, he heard the whistle go.

'That's it,' he said. 'We've won the championship.'

He looked across at Dave and Tommy the scout. Could there be an even bigger prize in the offing? The Diamonds were celebrating in earnest until Ratso put a dampener on the proceedings.

'I hate to tell you this,' said Ratso. 'But it isn't all over yet.'

'What do you mean? Longmoor haven't got back into it, have they?'

'Oh no, Ajax are murdering them.'

'So what's the problem?'

Suddenly Kev saw the problem. Dark horses Ajax could still pip them to the title. It was all a matter of goal difference. The Diamonds rushed across to watch the dying moments of the Longmoor-Ajax showdown.

'What's the score?' panted Kev to the Ajax substitute Billy Nuttall.

'Five-one,' said Billy.

Kev stared at Ratso. 'Well?'

'Hang on,' said Ratso, scribbling furiously on a scrap of paper. 'Let's see, yes, if Ajax win by five clear goals they're champions instead of us.'

'Oh, you're joking,' said Kev. 'That means if they score again we come second.'

Ratso nodded.

'Come on, ref,' Kev pleaded. Blow, will you?'

But Ajax's Barry Cameron was surging forward.

'I don't like the look of this,' said Conor.

Cameron beat one man, turned inside a second and fired in a shot.

'I can't look,' said Ratso.

What Ratso missed was the sight of the ball heading goalwards, bending sweetly just inside the left-hand upright. What he also missed was Longmoor keeper Jonathan Wright palming it on to the post and out for a corner.

'You can open them,' said Daz.

But Ratso preferred to keep his eyes shut, sparing the sight of the corner thudding against the crossbar. After a furious melee in the Longmoor area, Gerry Darke finally cleared his lines. He was determined to make sure the scoreline didn't get any more embarrassing. When the final whistle went the Ajax players looked around, wondering if their goal-spree had been enough. But the sight of the Diamonds mobbing Ronnie told them they had just missed out.

'Champions,' roared the Diamonds. 'Champions.'

Ratso did his calculations again.

'There's no doubt about it,' he announced gleefully. 'We've done it. Our goal difference is superior by one single, solitary goal!'

'That's enough,' said Kev. 'We've done it, lads. We've actually done it.'

That's when he saw Brain Damage and Costello sneaking away.

'Hey Costello,' he called. 'Good penalty.'

Costello scowled.

'What was that you said to me earlier? You called me a loser, didn't you? Well, look at me, now, Costello. This . . .' He drew himself up. 'This is what you call a winner. Got that, I'm a winner!'

Just how much of a winner he discovered moments later when Dave Lafferty caught up with him.

'Where's Tommy?' Kev asked.

'Gone.'

'Oh.'

Kev's jubiliation was slightly dampened.

'No,' said Dave. 'It isn't bad news. He's interested in two players.'

'Two?'

'Yes, Wayne Bowe from the Liver Bird and . . .'

The whole world went into slow motion as Kev waited for Dave to finish.

'You.'

'Me?'

'That's right, Tommy wants you to come down to Bellefield next week. I'll come with you if you want.'

'Everything all right?' asked Ronnie, approaching them.

'Oh yes,' said Kev. 'Everything is just brilliant.'

# Twelve

It was almost a week later that Kev finally got to see his dad. The moment he walked into the flat he was aware of something different. He couldn't put his finger on it at first, then it came to him. Dad looked smaller somehow and he seemed to have aged.

'Are you all right, Dad?' Kev asked.

Dad gave him a puzzled look.

'All right? Of course I'm all right. Why?'

Kev felt stupid.

'Just wondered, that's all. When do you go to court?'

Dad shrugged.

'Could be a while yet,' he said. 'But I'm going down.'

'Sorry,' said Kev.

Dad laughed humourlessly.

'What are you sorry about? I'm the one who torched the shop.'

'Why did you cover for Ramage?' Kev asked. 'He didn't do you any favours.'

'Simple,' said Dad. 'Tony McGovern doesn't grass.'

There had been a time when Kev would have been impressed by that. Now it just seemed pathetic.

'But why stick up for him? He's an animal.'

'I'm not sticking up for anybody,' said Dad tetchily. 'I'm finished with Lee. Working for him has just given me a load of grief.'

'You really mean that? You're going straight?'

Dad tossed back his head and chuckled.

'I wouldn't go that far,' he said. 'By the time I get out of nick, who knows what'll be happening.'

Kev frowned.

'Look, son,' said Dad. 'It's not like there's anything else I'm fit for. I've had it with Lee. He did sell me down the river. Even worse, he would have let old Gooly fry. But don't go hoping or expecting me to become some sort of saint. I haven't got it in me. Whenever they let me back out on the streets, I'll still need cash in my pocket and I don't know of too many ways to get it. Not legit ones anyway.'

'It doesn't sound like you want to change,' Kev said sadly.

Dad shook his head.

'Maybe you're right, lad. Anyway, how's Carol?'

'It looks like the move's going ahead,' Kev told him. 'Plod's doing my room up.'

'Yes? What's he putting up – truncheon wallpaper?'

'You're living in the past, Dad. He's quit the police.'

'So when do you start calling him Dad?'

Kev snapped to attention. 'Don't be stupid. I won't be rocking the boat for Mum's sake, but I haven't got any time for him. You're my dad. Sure, there are plenty of times I've wished you weren't, but that's the way it is.'

'So you'll visit me inside?'

'You know I will.'

Dad patted the couch. 'Come here, I think we need a word.'

Kev ignored the couch and sat down opposite Dad.

'Kev, you know I've done some things . . .'

'You can stop right there,' said Kev, interrupting. 'If this is some speech about not following in your footsteps, forget it. Don't flatter yourself, Dad. I'll visit you in prison, but that doesn't mean I want to end up like you. No way.'

Dad looked startled for a few moments, then smiled.

'You've got an old head on your shoulders, son.'

Kev pulled a face.

'It's a wonder I haven't got grey hairs.'

'I hear you got a trial with Everton.'

'I'm joining their School of Excellence,' said Kev, correcting him.

'Think you'll make it?'

'Who knows?' said Kev. 'I'll give it a go. Mum keeps

telling me to keep my feet on the ground, try hard at school and all that.'

'Will you?'

Kev shrugged.

'I know,' said Dad. 'You'll give it a go.'

It was Kev's turn to smile.

'Anyway,' he said, glancing at his watch. 'I've got to go in a minute.'

'Why?' asked Dad. 'Where are you off to?'

'The Dockers' Club. We're being presented with the championship trophy this evening. Do you want to come?'

'I'd better not,' said Dad. 'Old Gooly will be there to see his son get his medal. I don't think I'd be welcome somehow.'

Kev nodded.

'I'll see you around, Dad.'

'Yes,' Dad replied. 'See you soon.'

George Rogan was well into his speech before Kev managed to put Dad out of his mind.

'Our first presentation tonight,' the League secretary announced, 'is to Ajax Aintree. Just yesterday they won the Challenge Cup by beating the Liver Bird in the final.'

Kev grinned to his team-mates. Ajax had trounced Costello and Co six-two and Brain Damage had been sent off for two bookable offences. The result had been icing on the cake. The Liver Bird received muted applause as they accepted their runners-up medals. The Diamonds led the much warmer welcome given to Ajax.

'I wonder if we'd be clapping like this if they'd pipped us to the title,' said Ratso.

'Of course not,' said Kev. 'I'm clapping because they stopped Longmoor in their tracks.'

Daz nodded vigorously. 'Me too.'

'And now,' George Rogan continued. 'It gives me great pleasure to award the League Championship trophy to the Rough Diamonds.'

Kev started to get up, but Ronnie gestured to him to wait for a few moments.

'The first time I saw these boys play,' Mr Rogan continued, 'they were getting tanked week in, week out. By the end of that first season they'd lifted the Challenge Cup. Now, just twelve months later, they've captured the League title. Well done, lads.'

Kev again started to leave his seat, but was once more advised to hang on.

'As a result of the team's efforts, two members of the original side, David Lafferty and Kevin McGovern, have been rewarded with places in Everton's School of Excellence.'

Mum and Ronnie led the extended round of applause.

'Kev,' Ronnie hissed. 'Don't just sit there. Get up.'

Kev led his team to the top table.

'Well done, Kevin,' said Mr Rogan, handing him the cup. 'And good luck in the future.'

Kev turned and raised the cup aloft. With a mischievous grin, he waved it provocatively in the direction of the Liver Bird. He was about to pass the cup to Bashir when he saw a wiry man in a leather jacket hovering in the doorway. Dad, thought Kev, you came after all. Their eyes met for an instant, then Dad was gone. As Kev settled back in his seat, Mum leaned forward.

'Well done, Kev,' she said. 'You deserve it.'

Jack Dougan added his comment. 'Yes,' he said. 'Well done, son.'

Kev glared at him, as if to say: Don't call me, *son*. Then he was lovingly examining his championship medal.

'We did it, Kev,' said Jamie.

'Yes,' said Kev, fighting to control the lump in his throat. 'We did it all right.'

# Thirteen

*So that's it then. We finally proved it. We're the best. I always thought that would be it, I suppose. Once we'd won the title I'd start to feel different. We'd have rubbed Costello's and Brain Damage's noses in it, we'd have proved ourselves. The hunger that has gnawed at me for the last two years would finally be gone. It's not like that, though. Sure, I climbed to the summit. But it was only the summit I could see. Once I reached the top, I realized that there were other peaks, higher and more challenging, stretching into the furthest distance. The School of Excellence and maybe even a YTS with a top club at the end of it, a new house and a new life, maybe even a new me. Yes, I've come a long way and it's all change. I've mixed feelings though. Mum says I can stay at Scarisbrick now I've started to settle (her words, not mine!), so I'll keep in touch with my mates. That's about the only thing that will stay the same, though. Mum and Dougan are getting married in the winter, as soon as her divorce comes through. Dad's up in court next month so the only way I'll be seeing him is across a table on prison visits. As for the Diamonds, they're carrying on in the Under-14s, but I won't be there with them. I'll be playing all my footy for the Everton juniors. Daz is taking over as captain. He'll be good; he's certainly got the mouth for it!*

*When I look back over the last few years I sometimes wonder how I got through it. I've heard people – Mum mostly – say they'd love to live their lives over again and avoid their mistakes. Not me. No way could I do it all twice! The good things I've done, they're part of me. The bad things? Well, they're part of me too. Maybe I even learned a thing or two from them. What I do know is, I made a difference. The Diamonds will always remember me. I got a grip of myself as well. At long last I feel in control of my life. I really am the Guv'nor.*

Other books you might enjoy in the TOTAL FOOT-BALL series

### *Some You Win . . .*

'There's me with my mind full of the beautiful game . . . and what are we really – a bunch of deadbeats . . .'

But Kev has a reputation to live up to and when he takes over as captain of the Rough Diamonds he pulls the team up from the bottom of the league, and makes them play to win . . . every match.

### *Under Pressure*

'The pressure's on. Like when you go for a fifty-fifty ball. Somebody's going to blink, and it isn't me. Ever.'

Kev, captain of the Rough Diamonds, acts swiftly when too many of the lads just aren't playing the game and let pressures off the pitch threaten the team's future.

### *Divided We Fall*

'If you don't take risks you're nothing. There's only half an inch of space between determination and dirty play and I live in it.'

That's the law Kev McGovern lays down for the Rough Diamonds on the pitch, but what about off it? When Kev's best mate Jamie's world is wrecked by dirty play he's desperate to get everything back to safe, reliable normality.

## Injury Time

'Some people have all the luck. Dave Lafferty for one. How else do you explain a kid who's brilliant at everything? I would have given my right arm to swop with Dave.'

But Kev is stunned when he discovers that Dave has to cope with epilepsy. When he suffers a major attack, the victory the Rough Diamonds are so desperate to win, the longed-for junior league Challenge Cup, hangs precariously in the balance.

## Last Man Standing

'Losing's never fun, but sometimes you learn more from a defeat than half a dozen wins.'

John O'Hara is a midfield player for the Diamonds. Kev doesn't know what to do when trouble at home makes John lose form and credibility both on and off the pitch. His mind's just not on the game, and it's up to Kev to get him back on the ball.

## Power Play

'*What is* your problem?' asked Kev, starting to lose patience.

*My* problem thought Chris. 'At the moment . . . you. I want you and your stupid mates to get out of my face.'

The Rough Diamonds are a close knit team. Kev McGovern makes sure they work hard and play hard. He doesn't make any allowances. That goes for the new boy Chris Power who's just signed up with the Diamonds. Kev is determined to find out what makes him tick – and he does, but not until the very end, when it's almost too late.

## Twin Strikers

The Rough Diamonds have fought hard to claw their way up the league, but now they're struggling with injuries and loss of form. Talented twin brothers, Liam and Conor Savage, join the team. They ought to be the answer to all the Diamonds' problems – but could they turn out to be the biggest problem of all?